THE ARCHANGEL'S DEAL

K. REA

THE ARCHANGEL'S DEAL

THE ARCHANGEL'S LEGACY | ONE

The Archangel's Deal © 2022 K. Rea

The Archangel's Deal

The Archangel's Legacy | Book 1

Copyright © 2022 by K. Rea

No part of this book may be reproduced, distributed, transmitted, or utilized in any form or by any means, electronic or mechanical, including photocopying, recording, or by any information storage and retrieval system, without the prior written permission of the author.

This is a work of fiction. Names, characters, businesses, places, events, locales, and incidents are either the products of the author's imagination or used in a fictitious manner. Any resemblance to actual persons, living or dead, or actual events is purely coincidental.

To contact the author, please use the contact form on her website; kreaauthor.com .

Publishing Company Contact Information:

Kreative-Books, LLC

Bradenton, Florida, 34211

hello@kreative-books.com

kreative-books.com

Cover & Interior Design by Danielle Doolittle | DoElle Designs | www.doelledesigns.com

Editing by:

- CamRei Editing | https://www.facebook.com/CamRei.Editing
- Fluffy Fox Editing Services | https://fluffyfoxllc.wixsite.com/fluffyfoxpublishing

❦ Created with Vellum

DESCRIPTION

The Archangel's Deal

AN OUTCAST, AN ARCHANGEL, AND A DEAL THAT WOULD BE MORE THAN EITHER OF THEM BARGAINED FOR.

Nora would do anything to protect her sister and avoid the Pit—even take a deal from the one Archangel she despises.

When a contract goes sideways and Nora ends up in handcuffs, she takes an archangel's deal to escape a life sentence in the Pit, a literal hell on Earth for any fallen angel or wayward demon—but more so for the daughter of an archangel and human.

The Viscount Archangel of New Haven himself introduces Nora to the glitz and glam of the upper class angels. But not all is as it seems in New Haven, and no one is safe. Least of all, the angel halfling tasked with uncovering the traitors in their midst.

CHAPTER 1

*P*resent Day

"All that's left to do is sign on the dotted line, then we can proceed with your auction, Nora," Tomas said with a sly smile as he pressed one scarred finger down on the contract between us. He pushed it slowly toward me as he held a pen outstretched in his other hand.

"You know, it didn't take long for word to spread through New Haven. Demon-halflings are a dime a dozen, but the daughter of a fallen archangel—well, you're something special. There's already a crowd waiting to see you. We've even started selling seats. Honestly, your blood alone will fetch quite a sum. If you're willing to negotiate other assets, you'd make enough to go anywhere in the world and keep your little sister in luxury for years if you play your cards right," Tomas suggested.

I didn't need luxury. I wanted good food on the table, a safe roof over our heads, and maybe even enough money to go to flight school once Lyra's future was secure.

I cautiously took the pen from him with an unsure look. He smiled innocently back at me. I didn't trust him. Tomas had been after me to sign one of his contracts since my mom died. I never thought I'd actually agree to one. Still, desperation had a way of changing a person's limits of what they would and wouldn't do.

Tomas touted the dank storage room as his office when I arrived to sign his deal. The thin walls did nothing to muffle the murmuring of growing conversations outside, and I could already hear his eager clientele. Despite his efforts to elevate the room with an oak desk, a fancy chair, and trinkets, it was still just a storage room. He had an assortment of odds and ends stacked along the far wall on wooden shelves beside a massive safe. They were mostly demon and angel relics from the Arcadian war people used to barter their debts away.

Rain pounded against the warehouse roof outside, and I could hear the faint dripping of water from a leak inside. I stepped up to the wood desk and pulled the short stack of papers toward me. The white paper glowed softly in the dim room; the smell of fresh ink hung in the air as he set a second stack of papers down on the table. I looked up at him at the sight of a second contract. He was a sly business owner, but I wouldn't —couldn't—let him con me. Making a clean deal was too important. This wasn't just my life on the line, but my sister's too; I'd make sure she would never have to stand across from a man like this and make a deal.

"In case you change your mind about auctioning off all your available assets, I drafted another contract.

With a blood-only contract, you'll get forty percent of the last bid. If you sign this second contract, I'll grant you seventy percent. No one has gotten a deal this good from me before, and you won't find a better one," Tomas said as he settled back in his leather chair with a proud smile, as if he were doing me a favor.

He was.

Technically, both contracts were illegal and came with a lengthy sentence for anyone involved if the House of Lords decided I was more angel than human.

Yesterday

The crumpled piece of paper in my pants pocket weighed heavily on my mind. Another pink slip for the growing collection in my nightstand. This job hadn't even lasted long enough to cover the cost of the office supplies in the box I balanced on my hip as I shoved my key into the decrepit lock of my family home, a flat in a five-story walkup.

"Miss Evans, back so soon?" Mrs. Crowley, my landlord, asked. "I thought today was your first day at the agency on 52nd St."

I took a steady breath. "The position didn't suit. Mrs. Crowley, I'll have the rent payment to you soon," I promised, hoping she didn't hear the false hollow of my words.

"They fired you when they found out you're an angel, didn't they?" Mrs. Crowley guessed. "It's not like they could tell. You don't have wings like the full-blooded ones."

"Something like that," I said. "They asked me to leave after lunch without cause."

They fired me when my background check came back, and they found out I left that detail off my application. The temp agency never would have hired me if they'd known my father was a fallen angel. I used my mother's maiden name, but it didn't matter. Human resources found out, and security escorted me out without an appeal.

"Their loss," Mrs. Crowley said sympathetically, before frowning. "Dear, I think it's time we face facts. You can't provide for yourself, much less your sister. It's been two months since your mother passed, bless her heart. Your family is four months behind on rent. My wait-list for paying tenets is growing. If I don't have rent by Friday, I have to evict you and report you both to the House of Lords. This has gone on long enough. I thought they would have shown up by now and taken you in."

House of Lords—the archangels that ruled over us all. Those angels didn't give us a second thought, and that's how I liked it. They were the reason my mother died alone. They took away my father the day my sister was born. His crime? Falling in love with a human and producing offspring. The last time I saw my archangel father called Ramiel, three angels were dragging him from my mother's bedside as my newborn sister cried. I would have nothing to do with the bastard angels if I could help it.

"Thank you for your advice, Mrs. Crowley. I will have rent to you by the end of the week," I promised again as I shoved our apartment door open. If I couldn't get the money, my sister and I would flee in the night before Mrs. Crowley could send the angels after us.

My stomach grumbled painfully. The glass of water and an apple at lunch did nothing to stop the near-constant hunger pangs. I set my cardboard box on the kitchen table and walked to the fridge, hoping there was enough for Lyra and I both to eat tonight. The old, yellowed refrigerator hummed as I opened the door. It was as old as Lyra and the newest appliance in the apartment.

There was enough bread and cheese for a single sandwich and one apple. I left both for Lyra when she got home from school. The kid needed it more than me, anyway. She was growing like one of her weeds these days. Her plants, a motley crew of weeds, greens, and herbs, had taken over every window in the apartment. They thrived under Lyra's care, likely because she sang and played for them daily with her angelic gift, but salads only sustained us for so long. If only the rest of the apartment responded to her music in the same way.

The apartment walls desperately needed a fresh coat of paint. The radiator was spotty, and the lights flickered every time our neighbors turned on their televisions. But it was clean, dry, and I could pinpoint every item Mom made, found, or bought that made it home. Before she got sick, we never felt like we had less. What we couldn't afford, we made up for in other ways. Now that she's gone, I've never felt so lost.

I grabbed my favorite mug from the cupboard and filled it to the brim with tap water. Water would have to do for now. I filled it a second time, but before I could finish, the phone rang. A phone call was never good. I could count the number of people who had that number on one hand.

I picked up the relic from a decade past, an ancient corded phone mounted to the kitchen wall. The excessive cord dangled to the floor. I twisted the coiled cream wire around my wrist as I picked up the handset.

"Hello?" I answered.

"Hello, is this Ms. Nora Evans?" a feminine voice questioned.

"Yes, who is this?" A sense of dread settled in my stomach. I leaned against the wall and stared at the water-damaged popcorn ceiling. This day couldn't get worse, could it?

"This is Olivia Allen from Lyra's school. There's been an incident. Please come down to the school immediately. If you're not here within the hour, the principal will call the authorities," she said in a clipped tone.

"What happened? Is Lyra okay?" My exhaustion disappeared in a flood of worry for my sister.

"I can't say more. Just get here before the principal calls the House of Lords. Quickly, Nora, or your sister may not be here when you arrive," Olivia whispered before the line went dead. Lyra went to a human school. If she hurt a fellow student, she would be treated the same as any other fallen angel or demon.

The angels at the House of Lords were not known for mercy.

CHAPTER 2

Yesterday
I slammed the handset back onto the dock, letting the coil dangle as I dashed to the coin dish. After I grabbed the handful of coins and my keys, I locked the apartment and sprinted down the five flights of stairs as fast as my feet could carry me. If I hurried, I would just barely catch the bus headed to Lyra's school in the city.

Ahead of me, the bus lights flashed as it pulled away from the closest station. I ran. I ran with everything my starved body had left to give. I would not let the angels take Lyra from me too. They'd taken too much already. With my sides heaving and my lungs burning, I slapped my hand against the back of the bus window before it merged into traffic. The shriek of worn brakes rang out in the air as the bus came to a full stop. Blessedly, I heard the doors open.

"Get on with you, then. I have a schedule to keep, lady!" the bus driver hollered as I jogged to the front of the bus. The driver's annoyed look softened a little when he saw me.

"Where are you going, lady?" he asked briskly.

"New Haven Middle School," I gasped.

"That'll be four dollars and seventy-five cents. I can get you there in twenty minutes," he responded as he held his hand out for the fare. I turned the coins over in my hands. I didn't even have four dollars.

"Hurry already!" someone yelled from the back of the bus. The bus driver saw the coins in my hand, noted the lack of a purse, and frowned.

"Keep it and sit down. I can get you as far as St. Posy Avenue. You'll have to walk the rest of the way," the bus driver said.

He closed the door behind me and pulled back onto the road. I sat and willed my breath to slow. Two stops later, and more than a few snide remarks from passengers, the bus driver looked back at me.

"Lady, this is your stop," the bus driver said.

"What time is it?" I asked as I rose from the worn plastic seat.

"Quarter to four. Another bus doesn't come for thirty minutes. Now go on and don't hit my bus again. Best of luck to you. You look like you need it," the bus driver said kindly before waving me off his bus. St. Posy Avenue—ten blocks from Lyra's school. I started running again. The half-mile was packed with pedestrians. New Haven was always busy until sunset.

With relief, the rust-colored brick steps of Lyra's school came into view before too long. I took them two at a time. At the top stood a woman checking her watch with a frown. Her bun was perfectly styled, her outfit perfectly tailored to fit the school's strict dress code. She looked vaguely familiar.

"Olivia?" I asked.

"Nora! Thank the lords. Follow me, hurry. There's no time," she said. She put her badge up to the door. The lock disengaged, and I followed her into the school. It had been almost a decade since I walked these halls as a student. I spent a fair amount of time at the principal's office, but that hadn't prepared me for the sight of Lyra. Tear-stained cheeks, trace signs of a bloody nose, and, worst of all, clutched in Lyra's lap was the harp our mother gave Lyra for her thirteenth birthday. A gift we couldn't afford, but Mom made it happen somehow, knowing it would be the last one she would give. Now the harp was smashed to pieces, only held together by strings and my sister's hands—a mangled pile of gilded wood and strings.

"Lyra!" I called and attempted to run to her side, only to be blocked by a burly man in a tweed suit. The mustard color was just as offensive as the man's cologne.

"Not so fast, Ms. Evans. We have a situation here," Principal Maynard said, his voice loud and inflated with his own arrogance. "Your sister attacked a student."

"That's not true! He pushed me, took my harp, and destroyed it! He destroyed it, Nora!" Lyra cried. Tears began rolling down her face again.

"That's enough out of you, missy. The adults are talking," Principal Maynard grumbled. I swallowed my spite.

"Where's the boy?" I asked calmly. Maynard smiled.

"He's in my office. His parents are on the way," Maynard said.

"What did he say happened?" I asked.

"Leland, come out here. Ms. Evans wishes to hear

what Lyra did from you," Maynard said. Olivia moved next to Lyra and put a hand on her shoulder as Lyra cried further. The bullying had only gotten worse after Mother died. A young man emerged from the office. He held an ice pack up to his jaw, and a black eye was darkening his features. I did my best not to smirk.

"I was minding my business when that mutt—"

"Lyra," I snarled. He looked at me, then grinned. He fed off confrontation and relished in the power he had over us at this moment.

"Lyra," he said slowly, enjoying making my sister squirm, "tripped over her own feet, breaking her harp. In an angel rage, she attacked me, hitting me with angel strength and light."

The liar. I could smell and taste the lies in the surrounding air, that sickeningly sweet scent like spoiled fruit. Angel truth, my blessing, and my curse.

"Thank you, Leland. Please return to my office," Principal Maynard said. The young man smirked at Lyra before shutting the door behind him.

"He's lying. Lyra doesn't have angel rage; only archangels do. She's a child. She certainly doesn't have angel strength or angel light. We've been over this," I responded as I felt my fury grow.

"Yes, well, that may be, but those two had an altercation, and not for the first time. She admitted she hit Leland, a human. Per our agreement, when we accepted her as a student, she would be expelled for any misconduct," Principal Maynard responded.

"What about the boy? Is he expelled? Is he going to replace her harp?" I snapped.

"Expelled? Replace her harp? Dear girl, if you're not gone by the time his parents arrive, you'll both find yourselves before the House of Lords. At worst, she'll be the youngest angel sent to the Pit. Now, take your sister and leave before I call them myself. A formal complaint will be filed with the House of Lords by the end of the week," Principal Maynard ordered. I turned to Lyra. She was struggling to regain her composure. Olivia held out a familiar worn blue backpack, patched over more than once since I used it. I knelt in front of Lyra, gently took the harp from her, and put it in the pack before slipping it onto my back.

"I'll walk you out," Olivia whispered. The school's double doors closed behind us before she said another word.

"Lyra, why don't you wait at the bottom of the steps? I'd like a word with your sister," Olivia asked. Lyra obeyed without protest. She was always the better behaved of us.

"I saw what happened, and Leland is lying. His parents paid to keep him at this school. Maynard won't stand against them, even though your sister is a model student. He attacked her and broke her harp. I know how much it meant to her. There's a music shop on 57th St., I don't know if they can repair it, but they might give you a good deal on a replacement. Her gift shouldn't be wasted. Here's my number if she needs a reference for another instructor, and hopefully enough to cover bus fare for you both. Best of luck to you two, and I'm so sorry, Nora," Olivia said as she pushed a wad of paper and money into my hand, then disappeared back into the school.

Lyra was silent the entire bus ride home. No one gave us a passing glance. They were all too absorbed in their own lives to notice the devastated girl.

Five flights of stairs later, I spotted a bright red piece of paper taped to our door. Mrs. Crowley had officially given notice of our eviction if we did not pay rent by the end of the week. I ripped it down and opened the door.

"Are they going to take me away, Nora?" Lyra asked. She looked up at me, her eyes full of fresh tears again.

"No, dearheart, I won't let them," I responded. I wrapped my arms around her and squeezed her tightly in a hug.

"You promise?" she asked, and wiped the tears away.

"I promise," I said. Her green eyes, the same as mine, brightened with hope. "I'll take care of us. We'll be alright, you'll see. I'll make us dinner. Do you want to go take a shower and change into pajamas?" I asked Lyra gently. She nodded and left for the bathroom while I made quick work of her sandwich. I set it out with a side of peanut butter and the last apple. I made two cups of chamomile tea for us both—Mom's favorite—then called Tomas. The phone rang three times.

"Tomas," a gruff voice responded.

"Any jobs right now?" I asked hopefully.

"Temp job didn't work out, did it? Never does. I don't have any jobs that match your normal skill set," Tomas responded. The sound of papers being shuffled around echoed in the background. I took a deep breath as I heard the shower kick on across the apartment.

"Is there still a market for angel blood?" I asked. The sound of paper shuffling stopped.

"Are you in trouble?" Tomas asked. He almost sounded concerned.

"I need cash," I admitted, swallowing my pride. It was just blood. What's the worst that could happen?

"I can find a private buyer by next Saturday," Tomas offered.

"No, I need cash by tomorrow," I said.

"It'll have to be a public auction then. You won't be able to hide after this. More than a few people will know who you are," Tomas warned. "You'll have a target on your back in this city."

"I don't have a choice," I declared, staring at the last bit of food we had in the apartment. I was born in the shadows of the city. One auction wouldn't change that. The shadows were home, and they always would be. The angels could preen in the light, where demons were more than suited to the darkness.

"Ah, lass, we all have choices. We just don't like them. Be at the warehouse by five p.m.; the better you look, the better it'll go," Tomas suggested. "You'll need to sign a bit of paperwork and don't bring your sister. The auction is no place for a child."

*P*resent

"My safety is assured?" I asked, pausing before putting my pen down to sign beside my name. The cheap plastic in my hand was a catalyst for a choice I couldn't revoke. If you made a deal with Tomas, you kept it, or you were never seen alive again once he and his goons caught up to you. He was fair, but ruthless.

"As much as it can be. I had the boys turn away some of our less savory clients at the door, despite the size of their pockets. There's a mix of humans, angels, and demon-spawn out there. If anything happens to you, your payout doubles and is put in a trust with the bank you selected until your sister is eighteen," Tomas recited. I double-checked the bank and the account number he had listed on the paperwork.

The account I opened in Lyra's name earlier today at New Haven Bank was listed. It had the last bit of money we had to our names.

"The advance?" I asked.

"We've already written the check to cover four months' rent. Micheal is standing by to deliver it to Mrs. Crowley the moment you sign," Tomas said, gesturing to the tall, blond man standing by the door. He was a wall of muscle and the only man working for Tomas I trusted. Micheal and I had grown up together; he protected me more than once from the monsters that lurked in the darkness. Micheal pulled the check out of his breast pocket and winked at me before tucking it away again.

"I'll see it is taken care of, Nora. I fronted the advance," Micheal said. I could trust him with that, but I'd never trust him with my heart again. That was a hard lesson to learn.

"Thanks, Michael," I said. I leaned down to put pen to paper. The dress Tomas insisted I wear pulled tight across my shoulders and rose in the back whenever I leaned forward to look more closely at the contract.

A knock sounded at the door. Startled, I dropped the pen, and Tomas cussed as one of the most attractive men I had ever seen walked in. He quickly pushed past Micheal without an issue. Tomas jerked his head at Micheal, who slipped out the door behind the stranger, likely to fetch back up. Tomas always preferred the numbers be on his side, no matter the bid. He was a master of deals and circumstances.

That's how he got the name Bookie of East Haven. Tomas was the best at what he did.

The stranger was dressed in a crisp black suit, with his burgundy and gold wings pulled in tight against his back. The angel scanned the room with a scowl. With barely a glance at Tomas, his hazel eyes paused when he saw me. His fiery gaze trailed down my body, along the nearly sheer gauzy white dress Tomas assured me would help my blood fetch the best price. I felt ridiculous and exposed. I spent my life hiding, doing my best to go unnoticed; yet, here was an angel no one could ignore—tall, dark, and furious.

"Just the little angel I was looking for. You're coming with me," he ordered, his eyes flashing with a touch of annoyance. He was attractive—most archangels were—but also familiar, as if I had seen him before. I couldn't have, though. I hadn't seen an angel or archangel like him this close since the day my sister was born. My sister's birth was the only time I had seen an archangel, other than my father and his oldest friend, come to our side of town. Humans and halflings alike were beneath angels. Sure, some made an effort to help humanity from time to time, but it was a drop in the bucket compared to the damage caused by the Arcadian wars. They were our lords; we were merely allowed to live at their beck and call. Demons treated us more like equals.

"We're in the middle of a business transaction, sir. If you're here for the auction, you'll need to step outside and wait with the others," Tomas said as he rose from the desk and pushed a stack of papers toward me. The angel frowned and glared at one of the toughest men I knew. Tomas didn't flinch. He wasn't used to backing down from anyone—demon or angel. He was a dangerous but valuable friend to have. Well, maybe not a friend, more like an employer.

"Don't sign that contract. You'll be in far more trouble if you do. You can still come back from this," the angel warned.

"Who are you to tell me what to do?" I responded as I picked up the pen, pointing at him with it. He smirked, light reflecting off his wings as he shifted—burgundy and gold wings, the wings of a warrior.

"If you need a name you can call me Kass," he said as he scanned my body again in interest. "Based on that mop of blond hair and those green eyes, you're Ramiel's eldest daughter, Nora Evans. You're not signing that contract, and you're leaving with me now before this gets out of hand."

I turned and grabbed the paper closest to me and signed my name along the bottom line before throwing down the pen. Kass growled as I moved to exit the room for the stage. He reached out and grabbed my arm with a hot, firm grip as I passed.

"That was a mistake," Kass said, his eyes fierce as if they could burn a path right into my soul. Tomas walked up to us as I wrenched my arm out of Kass's grip.

"A deal has been struck, so a deal must be honored," Tomas declared, invoking the honor enchantment archangels had constructed to control fallen angels and demons. It prevented the demons from destroying humanity ten times over. Still, unexpectedly, angels were subject to it too—even half-angels. I felt the weight of the honor enchantment settle across my shoulders for the first time in years. Tomas had never used the enchantment on me before. Kass stiffened, stepped back, and crossed his arms.

"Angels can't break their deals, not even half-angels, and certainly not with me. We have an auction to conclude, sir. If you want sweet Nora's time, you'll have to bid like everyone else. I suggest you keep your hands to yourself," Tomas said, a bit too cheerfully. "Nora, you'll get your seventy percent after services have been rendered."

"Seventy percent?" I asked. "We agreed to forty for my blood."

"For your blood, sure, but you didn't sign that contract, sweetheart," Tomas said with a satisfied smile.

CHAPTER 3

"The contract you signed was for all your assets. You made the right choice, Nora. Now boys, get Ms. Evans on stage," Tomas said. His hands firmly gripped around that damning contract as his goons grabbed my arms and pulled me along a constructed hallway to the stage. Kass glowered behind him, but he didn't move. A deal struck; a deal honored—the one rule of New Haven that never changed.

"No! I didn't mean to sign that one. I only want to auction my blood, not my body!" I protested, trying to yank my arms from the goons' grip. They only tightened their hold as the enchantment burned across my shoulders.

I recognized both men. They were Tomas's shadows on gigs I'd helped with before. Travis and Gavin? Todd and Gabe? It didn't matter what their names were; they weren't letting me go. Both men just continued forward down the hall, taking me with them as if they hadn't heard a word I said. Tomas probably paid them well not to pay attention to anything anyone ever said, or maybe their consciences wouldn't let them.

"You should have checked the contract before you signed it," Tomas quipped.

"You switched them when I wasn't looking!" I hissed.

"You still signed it, sweetheart. The deal is struck. The ink is already dry. Even if you could break the oath, you know all my arrangements default to your next of kin, Lyra. Don't worry, sweetheart. It won't be so bad. After all, it's only for a fortnight," Tomas said.

"Fourteen days!" I cried. Regardless of my pleas, the men ushered me along, forcing me to move with them. The more I resisted, the more the angel oath burned along my back. A small taste of what purgatory would feel like if such a place even existed for half-angels.

"Think of your sister. This will set you both up for life," Tomas said. There was no hint that he lied, as much as I wanted to feel, smell, or taste any telltale sign of a lie. I cursed and tried to kick at him as his goons shuffled me along. "Some angel you are." Tomas grinned.

Then we were on stage. A simple black construction of painted wood, illuminated by a dozen stage lights. It was impossible to see the crowd. They saw me, though. Their chatter rose to a fevered pitch as the goons thrust me into the light. They guarded my back, and there was no way I'd make it through the crowd if I tried to run. I was stuck, angel oath or not. I would have to endure the auction and escape afterward.

"Ladies and gentlemen of New Haven, thank you for joining me on this special evening! Do I have a special treat for you tonight? I certainly do! Before you is Nora Evans, daughter of the fallen Archangel Ramiel. After much convincing, she has agreed to auction all her delights to you—her skills, her blood, and her body!" Tomas said. He was in his element now and operated like a true showman selling his wares.

The crowd raged. It became clear there were multiple demons among the many onlookers, along with human scientists, spectators, and the occasional angel. I saw Kass enter the spectacle of the audience unnoticed and lean against a wall. The fury in his hazel eyes glowed in the dark. Otherwise, he melded into the shadows, disrupting no one around him. The heathens were all focused on me.

"Now, she may look human, but she is half-angel. She has divine gifts and is untouched. Am I right, sweet Nora?" Tomas asked. "Something to do with a rash, innocent deal that went awry?" The crowd roared.

"That's none of your business," I said as I clenched my hands into the stupid angelic mockery of a dress he had me put on. It was at least two sizes too small and nearly transparent in this light. He had hoped for this outcome all along. Tomas probably paid the angel that interrupted us to come in and distract me so he could switch the contract out. He knew he couldn't get away with lying to my face. I dropped my hands and glared at Tomas as he winked at me.

"There you have it, ladies and gents. This poor damsel in distress needs all the help she can get. She came to me in need. You know good ol' Tomas is not a man to turn a damsel away. We'll start the bidding at ten thousand dollars!" Tomas said, his smooth voice amplified through the microphone. Then chaos started as everyone tried to outbid the others. A stream of numbers flowed out of Tomas's mouth as he responded to the cacophony of noise from the audience.

"Ten thousand to the human in the front!" good ol' Tomas responded with gusto. "Come on, folks! We don't have an angel like this every day! We may never again see such chaste divinity on this stage," Tomas crooned into the microphone. I scanned the dark room for an exit, any exit. There were at least fifty people between me and the front door. "There we go! Twenty thousand to the demon! Forty thousand to the human. Ladies and gents, you'll never get another chance like this!" Tomas said.

He loved this; he thrived off it. The numbers kept climbing as new bidders joined in.

"Eighty to the angel in orange," Tomas said, nodding his head. He began pacing back and forth across the stage as he saw folks raise their white paddles. There were flickers of white in a sea of black as they bid on me like heathens while I paced back and forth on the cheap stage. The goons kept their watchful eyes on me, but the angel oath kept me compliant. Fear for Lyra's future and my own added its own incentive to stay the course. No matter the outcome for me, she would be taken care of, and that was all I could offer her now. To buy her a chance at a fulfilling future, even at the cost of my life.

"One hundred to the demon with three horns! This is angel blood we're dealing with here. Think of the possibilities! Cures for sickness! Fountain of youth! Enchantments!" Each word out of Tomas's mouth added to my frustration and mounting anxiety. I did not want to be a demon's plaything. I glared at Tomas, but he ignored me.

"One-fifty to the woman in the pink hat!" I looked into the crowd, hopeful that the woman looked kindly, and human. "Two hundred to the demon!" Tomas responded with a slight frown. I spotted the woman with a pink hat, but she did not raise her paddle. Instead, she turned and walked away, disappearing into the dark shadows near the far exit. "Anyone want her for a quarter of a million dollars? You know she's got gifts. What angel doesn't? She's honor-bound; don't you want her for a fortnight? Anyone?"

"One million dollars," Kass said. His husky, warm voice echoed across the crowd during the pause. The room gasped as a whole, then many grumbled and growled at their loss. Tomas grinned like a cat, as many folks threw their paddles to the floor in defeat.

"Lyra will be safe," I whispered to myself. I no longer paced. Seventy percent of one million dollars would set my sister and me up for a lifetime of luxury and privilege. We could go anywhere, do anything. Besides, Kass was an angel; how bad could he be?

"One million dollars to the angel on the wall. Anyone else? Going once, going twice," Tomas coaxed.

"Two million dollars," a growl rumbled from the opposite side of the warehouse. A demon. His eyes glowed red in the dark, along with the veins that showed from beneath the edges of his suit. Even the horns that grew from his head and curled back glowed like embers. It was as if he burned from the inside out, full of fire and embers.

"Two million to the Ignis demon," Tomas said, a bit startled. He clearly hadn't known the demon was here. "Anyone else? Going once," Tomas said. Sweat was showing on his forehead. For once, he seemed unsure of this whole endeavor. My heart stuttered. A fortnight in the hands of an Ignis demon... at least my sister would be taken care of. I wouldn't survive. He'd bleed me dry, suck down my soul, or kill me before the end of the contract was through. Some demons you never make a deal with, not if you want to live.

"Going twice—anyone? Anyone at all?" Tomas asked, a touch of hesitation in his voice. The crowd murmured and squirmed, but no one said a word. No one wanted to be on the wrong side of an Ignis demon.

"Get on with it, Bookie of East Haven. We don't have all night!" the Ignis demon yelled. Tomas was far more than a bookie, but that was how he had gotten his start, and the title stuck.

"Ten million dollars for the little angel," Kass said, and the crowd gasped.

The demon roared, flames erupting around him, and people screamed as they dove to avoid the fire.

"Twenty!" the demon spat.

"Forty!" Kass said before laughing slightly and shaking his head at the demon.

"Fifty!" the demon yelled and threw a metal chair across the room at Kass. People screamed as they dove and ducked to avoid the projectile. Kass merely smirked and caught the chair, one handed, with a single smooth motion.

"Eighty million dollars. Call it, bookie," Kass snapped as he set the chair back on the floor before adjusting his suit. Others around him gathered themselves and their belongings before returning to their seats.

"Sold! To the angel in black," Tomas declared without hesitation, even as the demon continued to rage.

"Maximus, you've broken your oath—by Arcadian

Accords, you are hereby sent to the Pit for your crimes," Kass said. The demon froze as his eyes grew wide in fear. Kass uttered an old angelic Arcadian language no angel or demon wanted to hear—a spell only an archangel could invoke.

"No!" Maximus screeched before flames engulfed him. The enchanted fire left nothing but a scorch on the floor where he stood.

"Come and claim her," Tomas said, holding out that infernal contract.

I knew one thing for sure—Kass was no ordinary angel, but I was likely safer with him than the Ignis demon. At least, I hoped so. Kass strode to the front of the room, and everyone made way for him. His burgundy wings, tipped in gold, swayed in sync behind him with every step. Kass nodded to someone in the crowd as he stepped up onto the stage. He plucked the contract from Tomas's hand with a frown. He faced the crowd and spread his wings in all their glory. I recognized the wings now as dread settled in my stomach. Those wings had haunted my dreams for years.

"Now, with this auction concluded, it is my pleasure, as Archangel and Viscount of New Haven, to announce that everyone here is under arrest for violating the Arcadian treaty," Kass announced.

Tomas swore and ran for the exit while Kass addressed the crowd. Kass—Kassian Oriel, the Viscount of New Haven, the Archangel in charge of the city. He wasn't the angel that issued the warrant for my father's arrest, but he had carried it out. He had been a sentinel then. I remember hearing the news when he took over as viscount shortly after. The city was in turmoil, but with a newborn and her grief, our mother kept us inside and out of sight as the city adjusted. Now, his rule was law, and no one questioned him. At least, not to his face.

I was in trouble.

"The Arcadia accords strictly forbid any selling, purchasing, or distribution of angel blood, body, or parts. Alpha team, arrest them all; humans to jail, demons and angels to the Pit for processing. And you, Ms. Evans, are coming with me. We have business to conclude," Kassian said.

Lyra. What is going to happen to her now? There would be no money now, not with Tomas and me arrested—who knew what Kassian was planning to do with me. Would he send me to the Pit like that Ignis demon? Gone in a flash of fire, and no one to know any better?

Kassian approached me, slipping that cursed contract into his pants pocket, and withdrew a set of handcuffs. Before I could protest, he grabbed my wrist, spun me around, and secured both my hands behind my back. The cold, harsh kiss of metal encircled my wrists. Chaos ensued in the crowd as the lights came on to reveal cops and angels flooding in through all visible doors of the warehouse. For the most part, the humans appeared to submit to being arrested with little resistance. The scattered demons and angels in the crowd did not go gently; they preferred death to the possibility of the Pit. Tomas struggled beneath two cops as they handcuffed him.

"Captain Connell, make sure he's tried to the fullest extent of the House of Commons' court. I don't want him out on the streets preying on anyone else," Kassian said to the two police officers.

"Yes, sir. We'll make sure the judge knows," the

taller cop responded as they yanked Tomas to his feet and dragged him away to the House of Commons. Kassian placed a hand on my shoulder and turned me back to face him, despite the chaos going on around us.

"Time to go, little angel. We have much to discuss," Kassian said before turning me to the back of the stage and leading me through the hallway I had just struggled to get away from. He opened a side door I didn't see before, which opened onto the street. The sun had set, and steady rain poured from the skies. I saw a black limousine idling at the street curb nearest to us through the rain. Not bothering with an umbrella, Kassian nudged me forward. At our approach, the valet opened the backdoor.

"Thank you, Charlie. Nora, please get into the car," Kassian said. The valet moved around the limousine to settle into the driver's seat. The smile Kassian had when we first met was gone, a harsh scowl now firmly in its place. I felt the heat of his palm at the small of my back as he guided me forward toward the black leather seats. I slid in awkwardly, hearing the telltale sound of the dress rip before I settled into the closest seat with my hands turned toward the stoic angel. "Don't think about jumping from the car. Charlie has the safety locks enabled."

I heard a soft jingle of keys, then the pressure of the handcuffs on my wrists released. I scooted further along the leather seat wrapped around the cabin's interior. Kassian followed me and softly shut the door behind him. Rain pounded the roof of the car as he stared at me silently, assessing me again in the dim light. I shivered as the air conditioning kicked on. He clenched his jaw before shrugging out of his suit jacket.

"Take it. That dress is absurd. You're freezing and soaked through; you'll likely catch a cold at this rate, though that may be a mercy." He handed me the jacket, the fabric still warm from his body heat. I took it and slipped it on. It smelled of juniper berries, the forest on the edge of town, and an herb like Lyra's pot of lemon verbena.

"Thanks," I murmured. "What's next, Archangel?"

"What do you mean, what's next? How did you think this would end?" Kassian scoffed as he sat back in the plush seat designed to support his wings. He stared at me cooly, as if watching for any hint of reaction. "Charlie, take us to the Pit."

CHAPTER 4

The sway of the limousine came to a sudden stop as the gates came into view. The black wrought-iron gates were beautiful for such a nightmare of a place, as if the designer hoped to disguise the hell on Earth that was locked inside—the Pit. A vast yet simple concrete structure that was enchanted and reinforced to contain the world's demons hellbent on its demise, literally. As well as a few fallen angels along the way. In the Pit's history, none had escaped alive, though many tried.

Charlie parked the limousine outside of the gates in the night's pouring rain. We idled in silence as Kassian watched me. He was as much a predator in his own right as any of the demons in the Pit. Angels could have just as easily destroyed the world, but they wanted to rule it. He flipped open the fridge and pulled out three bottles of water.

"Charlie?" Kassian asked, holding up a beverage toward the driver.

"Thanks, boss," Charlie said as he caught the water

Kassian casually tossed at him before he raised the tinted privacy screen between the front seat and the cabin. Kassian turned to me and offered me a bottle. I took it gladly as additional lights flickered on around us, bathing us in light. He popped the lid on his own beverage and drank half of it before putting it down. He fidgeted with the signet ring on his left hand as he looked back at me.

"You seem keen on offers, contracts, and deals. I have a deal for you," Kassian stated as he leaned forward in his seat. More of that woodsy cologne engulfed me. It mingled with the smell of leather around us, intoxicatingly distracting because it was so different from the typical scents of New Haven slums and city streets where I had grown up.

"Depends on the deal," I whispered.

Kassian grinned and shook his head for a moment.

"Let me help you, little angel. This is the only offer you'll get on this side of the Pit," Kassian suggested. I squirmed against the buttery smooth leather seat and clutched the suit jacket closer around my shoulders, thankful for its warmth.

"What's your deal?"

"I've heard that Ramiel's daughters inherited his gifts. Is that true?" Kassian asked. I stiffened. We were never to discuss our true angel gifts with anyone.

"I don't know what my father's true gifts were," I lied.

Kassian frowned.

"We received a complaint today about a middle school student accused of angel rage and using angel light against a human boy," Kassian said calmly.

I seethed.

"That is a lie! Lyra is a child. She does not possess angel rage or angel light!" I hissed. Kassian nodded.

"I know. Pureblood angel children don't possess the power to harness angel light or angel rage. Only the strongest archangels do. If a halfling child did, it would cause chaos. I threw the complaint out and fined the parents for prejudice, but that does not change the facts. I was looking into your circumstances when I heard the rumor of a half-angel selling her blood in the East End. I wasn't particularly surprised to hear it was Ramiel's other daughter," Kassian said.

"So?"

"I had a lovely chat with Miss Allen, Lyra's former music teacher, when I called the school about what happened. She claims your sister has a gift for music, like her father. Our records suggest Lyra healed and saved your mother's life. Lyra has two gifts. Tomas suggested you had at least one gift. What are you capable of, Nora?" Kassian purred. The truth almost fell from my lips in an instant. I bit my bottom lip to keep from spilling all my secrets. He didn't need to know I was the one that healed my mother and sister with angel light, an archangel's gift.

"Nora?" Kassian prompted me. He crossed his arms over his chest and waited. The silence grew between us as I felt compelled to answer him. What was his gift?

"Angel truth," I said tersely. He relaxed and took a sip of his water. I was surprised he didn't push for more. Normally when I say I can determine the truth, most folks try to test me, not believing that almost every sense can determine a lie.

"That's what my source in the East End said. He left

some things out, but that bit was true, apparently." His voice was light. He sounded pleased.

"Who's your source?" I asked hesitantly. Few people knew of my gift for truth outside of Tomas's circle. My gift was a relatively well-kept secret. Or so I thought.

"That would be telling," Kassian responded, waving his hand as if dismissing my question altogether. "It's clear we didn't keep close enough tabs on you, though."

I glared at him. The idea of someone in the East End being in the angels' pockets to spy on my sister and me turned my stomach. Mrs. Crowley? My neighbor in 54B? Micheal? In the end, it didn't matter, did it? I was still sitting in a torn, borrowed dress in an archangel's limousine outside the gates of the Pit. Those gates were all that stood between me and a hellish existence at this rate.

"I need a person with your gift to solve a problem. Someone in New Haven is trying to undermine me and is working with demons. My deal is this: you honor the terms of the contract I paid for, but instead of a fortnight, you have a year to solve my problem. You will stay in Arcadia Tower. You will work at my businesses or at my side when I tell you. You will obey every order and command, and tell me who is truthful and who is not. You have one year to uncover who the traitor is and figure out what their end goal is. If you fail, try to doublecross me, or flee, I'll drop you into the Pit myself," Kassian explained with a hard smile and clenched teeth.

"The money?" I asked, and Kassian frowned.

"What about the money?" Kassian asked, affronted and turning away from me.

"The only reason I took the deal with Tomas was

for the money. I only meant to sell my blood so I could take care of my sister," I responded, ignoring the shame that threatened to color my face. Doing what needed to be done for the ones you love was nothing to be ashamed of. The deal I made wasn't supposed to hurt anyone, only save us and give us a future full of music and blue skies. Lyra deserved that, *we* deserved that.

"You ended up selling more than that, didn't you? Either contract was a criminal offense, as honorable as your intentions may have been. Frankly, your intentions are the only reason you're not already in the Pit. The Pit is full of demons, Nora. The demons rule there unchecked. They don't tolerate angels for very long. Most don't last without giving up their souls, their wings, or battling day in and day out. A half-human angel like yourself likely wouldn't last the night. They don't value honor and honesty like I do. Take my deal, Nora. It's the best one you'll get all night," Kassian said with a scowl. I glared back.

"I don't make deals with archangels that betray their own," I responded. I turned to the humans for help for a reason. I didn't trust angels to look after my sister. If I was in the Pit, she would have to find her own way, though. I opened my mouth to advocate for her, but stumbled over my words. I wasn't sure where to start. Kassian interrupted me.

"Being the daughter of a traitor, I shouldn't have expected more from you, but I'll sweeten the deal since money seems to matter to you. Deliver the traitor, or traitors, within the year, and I will give you half a million dollars to start anew in New Haven or another city of your choice. If you find them in a fortnight, I'll give you ten million. We can discuss the specifics if it comes to that," Kassian said before he finished the bottle of water, crushed it in his hands, then tossed it into a recycle bin built into the limousine wall. I looked down at my half-finished bottle and took another sip, considering his deal. It wasn't so different from my working relationship with Tomas. Except I'd have somewhere to live and food to eat, in theory. The Pit sure as hell wouldn't be as comfortable.

"What about Lyra? What happens if I don't find the traitors in a year?" I asked. I realized my hands ached from clenching his blazer between my fingers. I loosened them slowly as Kassian chuckled at my questions.

"Then I'll likely no longer be in charge, or dead. You'd have to plead your case with the next Viscount. I doubt you'll get such an offer from anyone else," Kassian said calmly, even as he spun the signet ring on his finger and his gaze wandered. Someone else being Viscount, or the idea that someone would kill him, had definitely gotten under his skin.

"What about my sister if that happens?" I questioned. Kassian stopped fidgeting, looked me straight in the eyes, and leaned toward me with undoubted certainty in his gaze.

"She'll be taken care of like any other angel child in the city, regardless of our deal," Kassian responded.

"What does that mean? I've never met angel children. For all I know, you don't have any," I responded. He laughed in response.

"Angels have children, just rarely. Lyra will have a roof over her head, all the food and material goods she could want, as well as proper training and education suited to her abilities," Kassian explained. "She will attend a boarding school with other angels her age.

She will learn to master her gifts, and will be taken care of."

"I accept your deal," I said steadily before downing the rest of my bottled water. I could have used something stronger than water. Kassian leaned forward and tapped on the glass divider between the driver and our cabin. The divider rolled down.

"A deal has been struck; a deal must be honored," Kassian said, staring into my eyes. His hazel eyes flared for a moment with angel power as the deal bound us. We would both have to uphold our part. He reached into his pocket and pulled out the contract I signed earlier.

"You never asked," Kassian said as he looked at me questioningly.

"Asked what?"

"What my gift is," Kassian said.

"It doesn't matter. You're an archangel; you're all the same," I scoffed, even though I was curious. I should have asked more questions. Maybe he had the power to manipulate me and my emotions. The only hint he offered was a bemused smile before the contract in his hands went up in flames. Angel flame, second to angel rage, the likely reason he was the Viscount of New Haven. Intricacies of angel government and their hierarchy weren't exactly focused on in human schools. Teachers were more interested in keeping their students out of the House of Commons' particular flavor of justice and functioning in society without demons' help.

"Little angel, you have so much to learn," Kassian teased. "Charlie, drive on. We won't be stopping at the Pit tonight."

"The next stop, then?" Charlie asked.

"Yes," Kassian responded as he settled into his seat. Soft jazz music played from the surrounding speakers, and I knew the conversation was over. We rolled through the city swiftly, the sights becoming more familiar until we were in my neighborhood. Charlie parked on the shoulder of the road within view of my apartment building, but did not drive closer.

Through the rain-streaked windows in the light of the streetlamps, I saw Lyra standing below an awning on the curb beside Mrs. Crowley and Micheal. Next to them stood two female angels in gray suits. The cardboard box I had used to pack up my office supplies was in Lyra's arms, but it was no longer empty. The tops of Lyra's plants peaked out from the top, and a familiar duffel bag hung from Micheal's shoulders. Men came out of the apartment complex with more boxes in hand and loaded them into a waiting van before turning around and going back into the building. A few of the boxes were open, and I could see our family treasures peaking out.

"You said you would pay the money and my sister would be taken care of! We're being evicted!" I hissed and tried the handle of the limo. The door didn't budge. "Tell them to stop!"

"Calm down," Kassian said coolly. "She's not being evicted. My associates are moving her out. She can't live there on her own."

"No! You promised; we have a deal," I responded and tried to find the button that would roll the window down. After a few fumbled attempts, the window finally lowered. "Lyra!" I yelled. Her head turned in my direction as a warm, masculine hand covered mine and pulled my hand away from the window controls. Lyra took a step in our direction before something or someone redirected her attention to the movers that arrived with another set of boxes. The window slowly rolled up, and with the slight tick of the window locks engaged. Kassian took my hand in his, gently urging me to look at him.

"Your sister is a ward of the House of Lords now. She will be safe, I promise you," Kassian swore solemnly. "She can't live in that hovel alone."

"It's our home," I said.

"It is being safely packed and delivered to the tower. I gave specific instructions to allow Lyra to take whatever she wanted with her. You both should have been in the care of angels from the start," Kassian stated. "After Lyra has adjusted to school, and if you honor your deal, I can arrange a visit."

"You're keeping me from her?" I asked, and pulled my hand from his.

"You can send her letters," Kassian responded.

I heard a bang that echoed the pain in my heart and pulled me from Kassian's fierce gaze back to Lyra. I watched as the movers slammed the other van door closed. The two angels in suits escorted Lyra to a white town car and ushered her inside, out of the rain. Micheal handed off the duffel bag and the box of plants he held to one of the angels. Mrs. Crowley waved to Lyra as the town car drove away before turning back to her building. The angel driving nodded to us as they passed, but I couldn't see Lyra through the tinted windows in the back. I watched until the white town car was out of sight, then I looked back at the apartment building that I had called home for the last twenty-three years.

Micheal stood alone on the sidewalk, hands shoved into his pockets as rain fell around him. He stared at the limo, but made no move to approach. He nodded at our driver, but didn't approach before he turned and walked away into the night.

"Micheal works for you," I whispered. He was the one man in the East End that knew my darkest secrets. The one man I had trusted fully.

"Micheal works for me," Kassian said softly. "And now, so do you. Charlie, we're ready to move on."

The limo pulled out into the street smoothly, and the only place I had ever called home disappeared into the shadows and rain before we turned onto another street. I angled myself away from the window to look at my new employer; the silence between us was a relief. For once, he wasn't staring at me. Instead, those hazel eyes were focused on the cellphone in his hand, another luxury Lyra and I could never afford. His wings rose above his shoulders, tucked in, but they still peeked from around his black dress shirt. Everything about him was tailored and trim, a warrior in a suit.

I should have recognized Kassian for what he was the first moment I saw him, but I naively ignored the signs. No self-respecting angel dressed like him would have been at a public auction to purchase angel blood. No angels should have been there at all. I should have run the moment I saw him, and Tomas should have known better.

Tomas. If he got out, would he hold me responsible? They didn't execute humans for angel trafficking, did they? Would he put a bounty on my head? A bounty wouldn't matter if working for Kassian got me killed or sent me to the Pit, but he could retaliate against Lyra to send a message.

Additional light from street lamps pulled me from my thoughts as we entered a nicer part of the city, where they bothered to keep trees trimmed and street lamps lit. With the rain pouring down, the surrounding city seemed to sparkle. It was clean and a far cry from New Haven's slums.

"Where are we?" I asked.

Kassian's suit jacket slid down my shoulders as I turned to stare out the window. The building we approached was massive and fairly glowed in the darkness, its white and glass walls a beacon in the night.

"The center of New Haven. That is the Arcadia Tower, our home for the foreseeable future," Kassian responded. The driver, Charlie, turned down a service road that led to a parking garage. He parked the car in front of a set of double doors with a guard on duty.

"Will you be needing anything else tonight, Kass?" Charlie asked.

"No, Charlie, that'll be all, thank you. Say hello to Angela for me," Kassian responded. The soft click of locks disengaging echoed around us.

"Good night, Kass. Good night, Miss Evans," Charlie said as Kassian opened the door and offered me his hand. He stooped low, his wings tucked in tight as he exited the car. He waited with one hand outstretched. He took his damp jacket from me and slung it over his shoulder.

"Good evening, sir," the guard said, waiting by the door and holding it open. I reached my hand out and put it in Kassian's. It was rough, warm, and strong as he pulled me from the soft den of the limo, out of some sense of safety and comfort, and into the unknown.

"Evening. Any news?" Kassian asked. His grip on my hand was sure and steady. He didn't drop it as he escorted me into the building in front of us, as if I could make a run for it. The honor bond weighed heavily across my shoulders at the mere idea. I sure as hell would not leave my sister in his hands unprotected. She was only half-angel and that meant little in his world. Though I suspected he was more honorable than most. Still, he was not to be trusted.

"No, it's been quiet since you left," the guard responded. "Is this the girl causing trouble down in East Haven?"

The guard looked human, but angels didn't always have their wings on display. Wings were a vulnerability unless they were airborne. It took me years to be thankful I wasn't born with any. I dreamed of flying. I wanted it more than anything else until they took my father away. Then, my lack of wings allowed me to stay out of the limelight until now.

The guard smirked at my glare before reaching into his pocket to remove a key pass, which he handed to Kassian.

"Here's the key you requested. Have her check-in with Sylvia in the morning to get an updated picture added to the system," the guard said before turning his back. He chuckled lightly. "Best of luck to you, sir."

"Good night, Marcus," Kassian said with a grin of his own. "Come along, little angel."

I followed Kassian through the well lit halls and down marble corridors. The tower reminded me of a financial institution or a courthouse, neither a pleasant feeling despite their efforts to decorate with plants and art. It felt staged and fake, though the decorations alone probably cost enough to feed Lyra and me for years. Otherwise, everything was bright and clean but cold, hard, and quiet—too quiet. The only sound I could hear was our own footsteps. We stopped in front of a pair of wood-paneled doors. Kassian held the key pass the guard had given him to a security panel. The elevator doors opened with a soft ding and Kassian waited until I followed him in to push the silver button for the top floor.

The ascent was silent; the elevator barely made a purr as it climbed the floors. Kassian shuffled a bit and flexed his wings slightly, almost as if he was uncomfortable in the tin box when he could have just soared the skies outside. It probably felt wrong, a machine lifting him instead of his wings.

"Floors one through nineteen are leased out to our corporations and businesses, which is where you'll be helping me. There is a cafeteria and a few restaurants open to the public on the second floor, and you're welcome to eat there. I programmed your key pass to allow you to go practically anywhere in the tower," Kassian said.

The elevator continued to climb as he went on. "Floors twenty through twenty-nine are related to the House of Lords and guest suites for visiting politicians and lords. The top ten floors are residential and recreation. Specifically, floor thirty-eight hosts an exclusive restaurant and bar where you'll be working most of the time," Kassian explained.

"Are we going there now?" I asked as my stomach twisted painfully from hunger. It had been far too long since I had eaten a decent meal. I felt disappointment keenly as Kassian shook his head no. We stopped on the fortieth floor, and the penthouse doors rolled open with a ding.

"You'll be staying in the penthouse with me. After you," Kassian said. I stepped out of the tin box in shock as the doors opened to a beautiful floor-to-ceiling view of the city. The sun had set long ago, and rain gently trailed down the window, but the city… the city glowed with a soft, magical light in a way I never imagined it could. The doors closed softly behind me as the high shrill of Kassian's cell phone ringing broke the silence.

"Excuse me a moment," Kassian said as he walked down the hallway to answer the call without waiting for a response from me. He stayed within eyesight even as I turned back to admire the city. From this height, it looked like a different world—distant, hopeful, and mysterious. I looked up at Kassian as the sound of his steady steps on the plush carpet grew louder the closer he got. He shoved his phone back into his pocket and approached the elevator. He held his wrist up to the panel, revealing a gold band. The elevator dinged, and the doors opened.

"I need to check in on someone. I'll be right back. Will you be okay here for five minutes?" Kassian asked.

"Yes."

"Good. I'll be back shortly," Kassian said, then darted into the elevator. The doors snicked shut, leaving me alone in a hallway with nowhere to go with a beautiful city view. I walked up and down the hallway, trailing my hand along the cool glass windows, trying to pick out areas of the city I might recognize, but nothing seemed familiar.

A minute passed.

Five.

Surely ten, but I had no way to check the time.

The elevator dinged, and an angel stepped off—one I didn't recognize. He had blond hair, striking cobalt eyes, alabaster skin, and was wearing a suit that looked expensive enough that it could have fed my entire apartment building for a month. He grinned at me, his eyes taking in my appearance. I'd forgotten about the ivory dress I wore, the tear making it more risque than it had been when I first put it on. The dress left little to the imagination before, and it certainly didn't now.

Wariness tingling along my arms, I lifted my chin even as I took a step back. The glass wall was cool against my back, and the hallway was empty. There was nothing here I could use to defend myself and Kassian still had my key pass, the only way to control the elevator.

"You must be the tainted trouble maker causing all the problems around the city," he purred as he approached me. I had nowhere to go and was stuck at the mercy of an unknown angel.

CHAPTER 5

"Tainted?" I bristled at the insult.
He grinned.

"You're Ramiel's brat. Well, one of them anyway. He always had a soft spot for human women, a weakness that got him thrown into the Pit to die with the rest of the fallen," the angel said.

"Better a brat than a prick. Kassian will be right back if you'd like to wait for him in the elevator," I said. One of his hands casually rested in his pants pocket, the other he used to loosen the black tie around his neck. Diamond cufflinks sparkled at his wrists, which matched a white gold signet ring—he was one of the Lords. Shit. His brilliant blue eyes flashed in irritation.

"Prick? Do you know who I am?" he asked with a tight-lipped smile. The edges of rage laced his words as he stepped closer, almost within arm's reach. He smelled of cigars and expensive liquor. He wrapped the tie around one hand like a boxer wrapping his fist. I kept silent despite how much I wanted to put him in his place. I knew his type—all talk, easy to anger, and swift to strike. Men like him didn't like their authority being challenged, and I didn't need any more trouble tonight.

"Archangel Mercurial Arisoso, Baron of New Haven." He paused, waiting to see my reaction. I didn't give him the satisfaction. That pretty face of his may have been unfamiliar, but that title was not. Mercurial "Mercer" Arisoso ruled the commerce district with an iron fist and a tendency for violence. He was one reason East Haven never prospered; at least, that was the word on the street. All money flowed to the angels in North Haven. The rest was divided between humans in the East and demons in the West.

"Did Kassian say why he brought you here?" Mercer asked.

"No," I responded. I could go left, right, or forward, but there was no more backing away from the archangel in front of me.

"Kassian always has a reason, always comes out on top somehow with his hands clean," Mercer sneered. "With your father gone, the House picked Kassian to guide the city. You would be nothing if not for Ramiel's blood in your veins. Just another human in this city slowly ticking your life away in some illusion of free will and simplicity. You'll never ascend, and will die like the rest of the sorry wretches in this city," Mercer said.

The Ascension, an angel's transformation from mortal to immortal, when archangels rise above lesser angels. Almost all angels ascend. Halflings, though, are more likely to die mere mortals—wingless, mateless, and at the bottom of the hierarchy. Neither human, nor angel, and rejected by both.

"You best watch that pretty mouth of yours, or your stay here will be very short indeed. I don't know what kind of deal you made with Kassian, but given how you look, I think it's safe to say he doesn't intend to keep you here for long once he's had his fill," Mercer said. "Unless he plans to share."

His wolfish grin suggested he was partial to the idea. Baron or not, if he took another step, I was going to barbecue his feathered ass. My father gifted me with more than one power, despite Kassian's suggestion that it was impossible. He and the rest of the angels could continue to believe their prejudicial lies for all I cared. I preferred not to show my hand too soon, but for Mercer, I might make an exception. Angel light could heal, but I learned long ago it could also burn like the sun in all its glory on a blistering summer day. I was more than ready to burn the prick, but I needed to keep a level head. I couldn't afford to anger every angel that crossed my path, at least not yet.

"No smart come back. Would you want that? Hmm, maybe you'll be here longer after all," Mercer said. He smirked and walked up to stand beside me, looking out the window at the city, or maybe at his own reflection in the glass.

"My wants are certainly none of your business," I responded. Mercer grunted at the affront. "If Kassian wants you to know what he plans to do with me or to me, I suspect he'll tell you... eventually."

"Kassian was reckless to bring you here. It will cost him more than he realizes. He should have tossed you to the Pit or let the highest bidder claim you for themselves. It will not please the House of Lords when they learn about your recent activities. Too many angels stepping out of line, leaving their bastard brats to cause chaos unchecked. This city has an opportunity, potential—same as you. Humans won't recognize it; they're a part of it. Don't waste your potential by selling your blood on the streets. With the right connections, you can make something of yourself. Go where angels can't, make connections that aren't open to us. If you decide you want to be more than a pet, come find me," Mercer said softly. He turned to me, those bright blue eyes analyzing me like a business contract or a prizefighter to bid on. It felt odd to be valued, measured and underestimated by so many powerful people in a single night. A part of me wished I had never stepped out of the shadows of East End, but for Lyra, I would do it again.

"I'm no one's pet," I responded.

"Perhaps not. Maybe come find me if you have any other ideas," he said suggestively.

I should have stepped away, put some space between us, but I didn't want him to mistake it for weakness. He reached out, trailing a silk tie-covered hand along the exposed skin of my arm. The touch was a cold, territorial, and utterly unwelcome advance. "You should know, I prefer actual angels in my bed, and you're a little too human for my tastes." A lie—a bold, sweet, disgusting lie that caused a shiver along my skin. I glared at him, ready to give him a piece of my mind and my fist. "But I've made an exception in rare moments." I missed the soft ding of the elevator opening.

"Should I come back?" Kassian's voice thundered in the hall, edged with irritation. He glared at us both. His eyes paused on Mercer's hand, my hair still in his fingers. "Mercer, I needed you downstairs in the meeting."

"Your new pet was lonely. I thought it best not to leave her alone to accost another unsuspecting man," Mercer said coolly. The false words fell from his lips effortlessly. Kassian frowned.

"Current events take precedence over a lone orphan angel. As this is my floor, my home, no one else lives on this floor, and she has no key—I doubt she would have gotten into much trouble if you hadn't come along," Kassian said. He stood tall with his feet spread and his hands clasped behind his back. Mercer dropped his hand and smiled at Kassian.

"I was looking for you, sir," Mercer said in a completely professional tone, but it did nothing to cover the simple deceit from me. What brought him to Kassian's floor if it weren't Kassian? This tower, for all its pretty decor, was definitely infested with at least one snake. Maybe I wouldn't be here long after all.

"Here I am. What is it?" Kassian asked. He relaxed his stance, crossed his arms, and cocked his head to the side. He didn't even spare me a second glance.

"It's a mistake keeping her so close. She's a threat. Give her to me. I can put her to work and house her somewhere better suited to what she is," Mercer said.

"No. If she's a threat to me, then I deal with it," Kassian said. "We wouldn't want her threatening anyone else. She clearly got under your skin."

Mercer balked at that before laughing. "She's not a physical threat by any means, but she'll make you look weak or corrupted. The others will talk," Mercer said.

"Oh, and what will they say?" Kassian asked, amused. "That I've grown soft because I didn't throw a defenseless young woman into the Pit to be ravaged by the demons we discard there? That she's bewitched me with her emerald eyes and insubordination? Or are you suggesting something else, Mercer?"

"For starters, why are you keeping her in the penthouse? She is beautiful in her own way, to some, I'm sure. I won't be the only one to notice. Especially dressed like that. Why bring her to the Arcadia Tower? She's nothing but a bothersome brat who doesn't know her place and should be thankful for the angel blood in her veins instead of trying to sell it on the streets like a harlot," Mercer said as he clenched his fists at his side.

"Enough, Mercer. Her place is yet to be decided. That is our fault. She is here to find a place for herself. Until then, she is in my care. Treat her with the same respect you would me. She's a fledgling angel, whether she is a halfling or full-blooded archangel. She has her whole life ahead of her. She didn't deserve to spend it in the Pit. You know as well as I do that we all make mistakes," Kassian said pointedly as he ushered Mercer away from me. They walked side by side down the hall. "Anything else anyone may say is the rumor mill and will die down with time. We have more important matters at hand."

"What's happened?" Mercer asked, his voice quiet, body rigid even as he looked over his shoulder at me as if suddenly wary of me overhearing their conversation. Kassian had no such reservations.

"There's been another demon attack on an angel stronghold. They tried to take a mother and her young daughter. The father came home in time to save the girl, but the mother is in critical condition. I need you to go check it out and see what the demons of West End have to say," Kassian said, his voice heavy with exhaustion, disappointment, and frustration.

"What of the halfling?" Mercer asked as he leaned closer in toward Kassian.

"She's none of your concern. Take care of the angels. We've called a parley with the demons. Police them if you need to. I've left Silas in charge until tomorrow afternoon. Report back to him and the assembly with your findings," Kassian said smugly.

"Silas? Why Silas? I have seniority," Mercer seethed.

"Because you weren't at the meeting, you were here with this little angel instead. Silas is already in talks with the demons," Kassian explained as he held his wrist up to the elevator doors. The elevator doors opened silently. Mercer strode by and glared at me before pulling out his phone. To my relief, the doors snicked shut, and the prick was gone, but the silence in the hall was almost deafening as Kassian looked at me. He covered his eyes with a hand before running it down his face. He was weary. Maybe the demon attack had affected him more than he let on.

"He's lying. I didn't proposition him," I said.

"I know, but he's not wrong," Kassian said with a frown. "Nora, come with me."

"Where are we going?" I asked.

"It's time we got you out of that ridiculous dress. Follow me," Kassian ordered, his tone full of annoyance.

CHAPTER 6

"Take that dress off," Kassian ordered as he ducked into a side guest room inside his penthouse suite.

"Excuse me?"

Kassian ignored me and walked straight into a large walk-in closet. He quickly pushed the doors open, revealing an assortment of clothes and a chest of drawers. Kassian opened one and pulled out a stack of soft gray fabric. He set it on a simple queen-sized bed covered in a white bedspread. The bedroom was nicer than any I had had the privilege of sleeping in, not that I had seen that many.

The room and everything in it was modern and sophisticated compared to the traditional, yet bohemian style I grew up with. Sleek lines and bold accents of gold, burgundy, and navy gave the white furniture and bed a distinct style. The room reminded me of the power and wealth the archangel before me possessed in spades.

"Change into these. I'll be just outside the door if

you need anything," Kassian commanded before leaving the room. The door shut behind him. Through a second door beside the closet, I could see an adjoined bathroom. I picked up the gray fabric, a set of soft pajamas, and carried them into the bathroom to change.

A hasty glance in the mirror told me all I needed to know about my appearance. I looked rough, wild, and wanton. The rain had mostly washed all the makeup that Tomas insisted on away. Some of my hair had dried in unkempt waves while the rest remained straight as ever. The white dress was worse than I realized. I quickly stripped it off in disgust and dawned the pajamas. The touch of the fabric was luxurious against my skin after being stuck in the cheap dress all night. The long sleeves and pants were a delight after being exposed for hours. I left my feet bare after washing my face and doing the best I could to tame my hair into some sense of decency. I left the bathroom to confront my host—my boss?—my *whatever*.

Kassian looked up at me the moment I opened the bedroom door. His pinched mouth turned up in a small smile and his furrowed brow relaxed as he took in my appearance. His gaze lingered on my bare toes before he cracked a smile.

"You don't have to go barefoot unless you want to. I forgot to mention there are socks and underwear in the dresser in the closet, along with an assortment of shoes. Everything should be in your size," Kassian said. He pushed off from the side table he was leaning against and began to walk away.

"How do you know my size? I just got here," I demanded as I crossed my arms and sent him a pointed look. He froze mid-step and turned back to me.

"We do our best to keep tabs on the East End and the dealings that go on. We heard about the auction from a few trusted sources and asked Micheal for information. He provided an in-depth dossier of information on you. We had hoped to avoid the auction entirely and host you here until other accommodations could be made for you and your sister, together, in a more private manner. Your decision to proceed with the auction forced my hand," Kassian explained before he cleared his throat. He was clearly still a bit put out that I had signed the deal with Tomas.

"We?" I questioned.

"My council," Kassian answered.

"Mercer?" I quizzed, surprised. Kassian laughed, the sound was jarring but a relief. Maybe we could get along after all.

"Gods no! He'd have you looking like an accessory to match his home. You'll meet my council tomorrow, one of which is Celeste. Celeste selected your wardrobe from her shops. I'm sure she'll love to hear what you think of it. We thought she was better suited to help your sister settle into school as well," Kassian said.

"Why is that?" I probed.

"Aside from the obvious? When she's not engulfed in fabrics, children and education are her passion. She helped create the school—" The growl of my stomach interrupted him.

"When's the last time you ate?" Kassian inquired, and a wave of shame washed over me. Kassian's eyebrows knitted together as he frowned at my silence.

"How long?" he pressed again sternly.

"Yesterday or the day before," I responded. He cussed.

"Follow me. Why didn't you say anything? You need to eat," he snapped at me and cussed again before turning and stomping down the hall. "I should have listened to Celeste and fetched you yesterday."

"Why didn't you?" I asked quietly, following behind him. The hall opened into a spacious, modern apartment. The themes of white, navy, burgundy, and gold continued throughout the penthouse.

"Celeste and I disagreed. She was right, though; she always is," Kassian admitted, his voice taking on a lighter tone as he pulled open a glossy black fridge and removed a mouthwatering assortment of food. With fresh vegetables, smoked cheese, and meat piled next to a walnut cutting board, he pulled out a set of knives and a loaf of rustic bread. Picking up one knife, he gestured to a bar stool beside the kitchen island. "She wanted to visit you yesterday before the auction," Kassian explained as he prepared and assembled a thick sandwich.

"You can usually get anything you want from the restaurants and cafeteria downstairs, but this should do for now," Kassian said as he pushed the plated sandwich toward me. I gladly took the sandwich.

"Is Lyra being taken care of like this?" I pressed before taking my first bite. I couldn't remember the last time I had a meal to myself without making sure Lyra had eaten first.

"Your sister will want for nothing while she remains at the school," Kassian assured. "Like we talked about, a deal was struck and that deal must be honored. If you don't trust me, this is going to be a lot harder on the both of us," Kassian said grimly. He opened the refrigerator and pulled out a bottle of white wine while I ate the sandwich. Kassian poured himself a glass. "Would you like some?"

"Sure," I accepted, while still enjoying the best sandwich I may have ever had. Kassian poured a smaller glass and set it next to the plate with the other half of my sandwich.

"Not my finest culinary dish, but I hope it's satisfying," Kassian said with a soft laugh before enjoying a sip of his wine. "Why didn't you come to us for help?" He took a seat beside me on the barstool.

"Almost thirteen years ago, minutes after my sister was born, I watched as you and other angels arrested my father and shattered my mother's heart. You had no mercy for the three of us," I said. "Lyra and I grew up knowing that a single shift in mentality meant that humans, demons, or angels could move against us. We were safer with humans than angels."

"It was a different time, a different regime. There was more to it than what you and your mother were aware of," Kassian said calmly. I waited for a telltale sign of a lie, yet there was none—no sickening sweet smell, no ill feeling or shiver along my spine.

"Regardless, first impressions and all that. I'm more likely to trust a human than an angel," I said before taking a large sip of wine. From the smell alone, I knew it would be richer than the single glass I had shared with my mother for my birthday. It was crisp and sweet against my tongue. The light bubbles were a bittersweet surprise as I swallowed. I set the glass down gently and picked up the other half of the sandwich. I ate this half slower, savoring each bite.

"The humans that just as easily lie to you, reject

you, betray you, abandon you, and force you into an angel-bound contract for money. Yes, I can see why they may seem like a safer option," Kassian said sarcastically, with a smirk as he finished his glass of wine. He didn't grab another. Instead, he reached for the bowl of red apples resting in the middle of the white quartz countertop. He bit into it without hesitation. A burst of sweet apple scent surrounded me, reminding me of home.

"It was always a risk. I thought too highly of Tomas. It won't happen again," I said gravely. The next chance I had, I would return the ill favor he did me. My skills had proven useful; I knew more secrets than even Tomas realized. If Tomas didn't spend the rest of his life in a jail somewhere, and I survived this business with Kassian, then Tomas's business would be in flames by the time I was done. The Bookie of East End would regret conning me.

"Our business arrangement will hopefully end on more amicable terms," Kassian asserted.

"Why do you think there's a traitor in your tower?" I questioned as I pushed my empty plate away and ran my finger along the stem of the wineglass.

"There have been demon attacks on my most profitable businesses—my angel allies, my outreach programs, and other targeted ventures only angels should be able to pinpoint with such accuracy. They have inside information. Someone is betraying me," Kassian said grimly.

"To what end?" I asked.

"In some ways, I think they mean to unseat me, take my title. I'm not tenured. The House of Lords can remove me if I'm deemed unfit. If that happens, I'll be bent out of shape for sure, but that's not what I'm most worried about," Kassian said before setting his half-eaten apple down on the counter. "What I am about to say does not leave this room. You do not mention it to another soul."

"Understood," I responded. The angel oath tingled across my shoulders.

"Someone is trying to open a door to hell."

CHAPTER 7

"Did you just say—" I started, but the angel oath stopped me.

"Someone is trying to open the gateway to hell, yes. At the very least, they're attempting to corrupt angels and make it look that way to incite panic," Kassian said. I laughed. The gateway to hell had been closed for almost two centuries. The very fabric of our society, the Arcadia Accords, was built on the one fact that it could not be reopened. Lucifer, his army, and son were locked away in their own realm, away from us. Kassian's grave face killed the humor, with no hint of a lie in the air.

"That's supposed to be impossible," I whispered.

"It's implausible, not impossible. You need the right combination of blood, magic, and sacrifice to open the gateway from this realm. The angels they targeted are descendants of the ones that formed the gateway. They're weaker and younger, but will still meet the requirements to reopen the gateway," Kassian explained.

"What would they have to gain?" I asked as the food settled heavily in my stomach. I was satisfied for the first time in weeks, but the idea of a gateway to hell being reopened didn't sit well. Kassian sighed and shook his head before looking me straight in the eyes. His were full of disappointment, anger, and wrath, though not directed at me.

"Why does anyone go to war? Chaos, wealth, power, glory? Do they want to free Lucifer or his heir? You are here to help me pinpoint who is doing this so I can put a stop to it before a war erupts. I fear we may not win a second time," Kassian said. The clock on the kitchen wall chimed softly, marking the hour. Kassian sighed. "We can pick this up in the morning. Will the guest room you saw earlier suffice?" Kassian asked.

"Yes," I said numbly, still trying to process the idea that someone was crazy enough to open a gate to hell. Kassian rose from his seat and walked across the living room. He pointed to a closed door facing the hallway.

"That is my room. If you need me, come to me. I won't bite," Kassian said, then smiled. "Well, unless you ask me to," he said in a barely audible whisper. "Almost anyone can access this floor via the elevator, but only three people have actual keys to the penthouse: you, me, and Celeste. Don't leave your key behind, the front door locks automatically. Tomorrow, we can get your key pass transformed into something more discreet that you can wear all the time," Kassian explained.

"How do you know I won't run?" I asked, still holding my wine glass.

"The oath you made, the fact Lyra needs you, and you have nowhere left to go," Kassian responded. I drank the rest of my wine in a single swig, not sure what to say. "I'll see you in the morning, Nora. Goodnight."

Without another word, the archangel with the future of the world on his shoulders, turned his back on me and retreated to his room. I set the glass on the counter and walked to my room. I shut the door behind me and turned the lock slowly, as if that would do me any good if he wanted to come in.

The penthouse was safer than the Pit, but for how long? Someone was trying to open a gate to hell, and I was supposed to help one of the highest ranking archangels find out who. A jail sentence in the Pit might have been better, but Lyra would have been worse off. This way, I could at least keep her safe for as long as possible and maybe stop a hellgate from opening.

A knock at the door woke me sooner than I wanted the next morning. The room was pitch black with the curtains drawn. I'd forgotten to leave a light on. Initially, I had a hard time falling asleep, but the side effects of a full stomach, the wine, and the most comfortable bed I had ever encountered pulled me in, coaxing me to sleep. I only hoped Lyra slept as well.

Lyra.

I tumbled from the bed, sheets and down comforter tangling about my legs.

"Coming," I called out. As I reached the door, I hesitated with my hand on the lock. No one had announced themselves and Kassian hadn't mentioned a wake up call.

"Good morning, Nora. Meet me in the kitchen when you're dressed. Celeste should have provided athletic wear. I recommend wearing it. We're stopping at the gym after breakfast before the actual work begins," Kassian's powerful voice sounded through the door.

"Okay," I acknowledged. I retreated to the closet, looking for the dresser he had mentioned the night before. It wasn't hard to find because it took over half the closet. I found the athletic wear he mentioned in the second drawer. A pair of sneakers were on the floor of the closet, along with several other pairs of shoes for any occasion: flats, heels, flip-flops, and a marvelous pair of black heeled, thigh-high boots. In the morning light, the contents of the closet were more visible. *Celeste picked a few things for you* apparently meant a more fully stocked wardrobe than I had ever owned. There were outfits and dresses for every occasion to match the tidy row of shoes. I promised myself I'd take a proper look at everything later and quickly dawned the athletic wear and freshened up in the bathroom.

Now in the proper attire, I walked into an empty kitchen. Kassian was nowhere to be seen, but a buffet of fruit and pastries was laden on the table. I grabbed a red apple from the centerpiece. I began eating it and inspecting a bowl of pastries when I heard footsteps coming from the living room. Dressed in black from head to toe, with his burgundy wings relaxed at his back, was the archangel.

"Should have known of all the fruit on the table

you would go for the apples," Kassian said with a smirk. I stopped mid-chew and swallowed.

"Why is that?" I asked, palming the rest of the apple. Kassian grinned as he picked one up as well.

"They're my favorite," Kassian said. "I don't typically share apples. Almost everything else is fair game."

"Oh," I whispered. Mercer's comment about Kassian sharing me with others may not have been a bluff like I initially thought. I swallowed the chunk of apple lodged in my throat with difficulty as I tried not to imagine what it would be like to be with a man like Kassian and shared with another. I looked away from him quickly to hide the flush in my cheeks as he chuckled.

"I meant nothing by it. You can eat as many as you want. I have them shipped in from the Arcadian mountains, a taste of home. I'll try to keep the fridge better stocked while you're here. I normally don't spend much time here," Kassian explained before grabbing a few more items, putting them on his plate, and sitting at a small dinette tucked to the side of the kitchen. I followed suit with a single pastry and hoped I wouldn't regret the decadent treat at the gym later.

"Why are we going to the gym?" I questioned as I pulled back a chair and sat beside him.

"Anything to drink?" Kassian asked before drinking from a glass of water.

"I'll get water later," I responded. "I didn't think physical fitness was part of our deal."

"It's not physical training so much as I need to see what defense training you've had... if any," Kassian said. "You'll have a target on your back just by being here and for what you tried to do."

"Great," I groaned. Kassian smiled.

"It won't be so bad. Some folks, like Mercer, will come to the wrong conclusions, but sometimes rumors work in a person's favor. I was thinking about what Mercer said last night. If folks jump to the wrong conclusions about you and me, it could help. We might help the rumors along here and there if you're game," Kassian suggested.

"Nothing crazy or vulgar?"

"Of course," Kassian responded.

"Sure, not like I have much of a choice," I grumbled before biting into the cream and fruit-filled pastry. Flavors exploded across my palate as Kassian frowned and put his breakfast down. His face stern.

"Nora," Kassian said, his voice deep and husky.

"In this, you have a choice. Deal or no deal, your body is your own. If you're ever uncomfortable with a plan or anyone's actions, tell me—even if I'm the one that caused it. To be clear, I need a partner for this to work, not a concubine." With a body and a face like his, I doubted he ever wanted for company. A halfling like me had nothing to offer an archangel like him except my special cocktail of conflict and baggage.

"Understood. I'll follow your lead," I said. Kassian nodded. A look of relief replaced the concern that had shadowed his face. I finished the pastry and pretended to lick nonexistent crumbs from my fingertips.

"That is if it's okay with you, sir?" I purred in a falsely demure, coy tone. Kassian laughed out loud and pushed back from the table. He walked right up to me. He put his index finger beneath my chin and tilted my head up to look into those blazing hazel eyes. He smiled, his finger moving to caress my cheek.

"Probably best if I make the moves, little angel," Kassian said huskily before dragging his hand slowly from my face. Remnants of cream and jelly stuck to his finger before he put it in his mouth. "Hmm, raspberry, another favorite. Come along, little angel. Let's see what other moves you have," he teased.

My cheeks flamed for a moment as he backed away from the table and turned his back on me. I followed him through the penthouse and into the hall that overlooked the city. Brilliant streaks of yellow, pink, and umber crossed the morning sky as the sun rose. The city glowed in the morning sun as if its rooftops and edges were gilded in flames. The elevator opened with the faintest ding. Kassian waited to push the button until I was in, and after a quick descent, the doors opened to a gym empty of people.

Inside was a standard collection of equipment, except for what appeared to be a boxing ring and an imposing door labeled as an armory. Kassian walked past those without a second glance to an area filled with bright blue mats and rested his phone and bottle of water on a row of cubbies. The air was bright with the smell of lemon cleaners and disinfectant, causing me to sneeze. He looked back at me.

"You'll tell me if you're coming down with a cold. We have healers that can fix you up," Kassian ordered.

"I'm not. It's the cleaners," I admitted as I smothered another sneeze.

"You'll get used to them, eventually. We prefer to keep everything clean," Kassian responded. "The doors to the left and right lead to the locker rooms. Your key pass will allow you into the training armory if you need any equipment you don't see here. Mostly dummies, single and double-handed weapons for recreational sparring. We keep anything that could do actual damage on another level."

"Don't trust me with pointy objects?" I teased.

"I don't trust hot-headed angels not to take things a bit too far. We keep our blood sports contained to less populated areas unlikely to cause a building to collapse," Kassian said before settling into a casual stance.

"Like where?" I asked.

"The sky, for one. The woods and the outskirts of the city, for another. Have you had any formal training?" Kassian inquired, his gaze taking in my stance with a frown.

"Not since I was little," I admitted with a shrug, a half-truth. Kassian nodded, considered my answer, and relaxed his stance even further.

I didn't have many memories of my father before they took him from us, but I remember the day he started teaching me defensive maneuvers. After he was taken, my mother found friends to finish what he started. Just because we weren't supposed to hurt humans didn't mean she didn't want us to protect ourselves or fight back. Cities were a rough place to get your start in life, and East New Haven was worse than most. Lyra and I were walking targets if anyone knew our backgrounds or caught us using our powers. I could still hear her voice.

"Run. If you cannot run, fight. Use your fists first. Use your powers as a last resort, Nora."

Her advice served me well over the years. She was a compassionate, kind woman, yet she still kept a 9mm in the kitchen cabinet in case someone came for us. Angel or not—she didn't care when it came to protecting her kids.

"Show me what you've got," he said confidently. I cracked my knuckles and rushed Kassian to see what he would do. He sidestepped my rush, a bit surprised, and swiped my legs out from under me—just as I hoped. I rolled to my feet and came up swinging. What I didn't learn growing up, I learned from hanging out at Tomas's fighting rings. No one fought dirtier and more savagely than men with their lives and money on the line. Kassian blocked my left hook, but my right uppercut caught him under the chin. He shuffled back with a shake of his head and a grin. Kassian rolled his head, cracked his neck, and his wings flared slightly before disappearing. He then brought his hands up to a more defensive position.

"Well then. Let's play, little angel," Kassian taunted. "Game on."

We circled each other, and he allowed me to play offense a little longer before turning the tables on me. Suddenly, I was on the defense. Always retreating, ducking, falling, and rolling away, barely a step ahead of him. I threw some of my dirtier tricks at him, but he kept his composure, never getting angry or frustrated. Yet, while I landed a few blows to him, he never struck me, merely tapped me or gently tugged on my ponytail.

Ten minutes later—or was it thirty?—I was breathing harder. A fine layer of sweat lined my brow and trickled down my back, but he didn't stop. He continued to push me, testing my weaknesses and providing suggestions.

After one particularly hard ponytail tug, I threw my elbow back, attempting to clock him in the head, only for him to duck and smack my ass. I reacted without thinking; I swung around to slap him across the face, except he was closer than I realized. His hand circled my wrist, stopping its arc before his other arm wrapped around my waist and pulled me close. He ducked his head down and kissed me.

It was soft at first, almost hesitant. He didn't dominate me, but waited for a signal from me. Any sign to suggest I was open to the action. I pushed my lips back against his, firmer and harder. Without a protest from my lips, he met my actions. The kiss became a fight of its own; who could give or who would take. His tongue explored my mouth, but he groaned first. My hands sought his shoulders, where his hands fell to my hips, holding me tight against him. I nipped at his lower lip as we consumed each other. He was the first to pause. As I struggled to catch my breath, Kassian slowly released me. He seemed just as winded.

"Kiss me just like that, little angel, and everyone will be too busy gossiping to question us twice," Kassian said softly before his hands fell away, but he did not move back. The warmth of our bodies was smoldering where they touched. I looked up and a flicker of emotion changed on his face until a ringing echoed around us, shattering the moment. He stepped back and walked over to where he left his phone on the set of wooden shelves. He was too far away to hear, but his posture suggested the call wasn't a good one. Before, he seemed relaxed. Now he was tense in an authoritative stance. He hung up angrily before looking at me, a glimmer of regret on his face.

"There's been another attack. I need to go. I won't be returning to the penthouse, but you should. Get cleaned up, make yourself comfortable, and rest. You'll start working tonight in the bar at my side," Kassian explained as he tossed me my key pass. "Are you comfortable finding your way back?"

"Of course," I retorted. He merely nodded; it was

clear he was preoccupied with the call. I pressed and waved my pass in front of the elevator. It opened, and I stepped inside, turning around to find Kassian watching me.

"Nora?" he started, throwing a hand out to stop the elevator door from closing.

"Yes?" I asked.

"Wear something that would make any angel consider falling from grace for you," he said before pulling his hand back from the elevator without another word.

CHAPTER 8

After showering, raiding the refrigerator, and sleuthing around Kassian's home, I took the longest nap I'd had the luxury of indulging in for months.

Settling into the penthouse wasn't as troublesome as Kassian's parting assignment. I spent more time sorting through clothing to wear than anything else. Two dozen outfits of the mysterious Celeste's choosing hung in the closet. Amusingly, the color scheme matched the apartment—burgundy, ivory, navy, and black items. I knew without a doubt I would wear the boots; I was half in love with them already, but I needed more than boots to make an impression—or at least the right one.

I wasn't particularly fond of the idea of being arm candy. I preferred to work in the shadows unnoticed. But if being Kassian's lady kept me alive and mostly overlooked, then I at least needed to look the part. I pulled out a short burgundy number and shimmied into it. The dress was revealing, with sheer billowing sleeves that went to my wrists and a plunging neckline that dipped almost to my navel in a narrow V-shape. Delicate gold chains lacing across the exposed cleavage kept the dress snug against my body. The hemline dropped to mid-thigh. Paired with the boots, I was less exposed than I was the night before, but still alluring.

I spent the better part of an hour digging through cabinets in the bathroom for supplies to curl my hair and put it into a sexy updo. After more than a few mistakes, I decided less was more with the new packages of makeup I had found. A knock sounded at my door as I was completing the finishing touches to the look.

"Hello, Nora! Are you ready?" a female voice sounded through the door. "Kassian is tied up at the moment. He sent me to show you the way to The Feather."

"Who are you? What's The Feather?" I asked as I reached for the kitchen knife I left on the dresser top.

"My name is Celeste. The Feather is Kassian's bar, where you'll be rubbing elbows with angels, demons, and the creatures in-between," the soft voice responded, a touch of amusement in the voice's lilt. "I'm here to offer my services and give you an update on Lyra. Would you mind opening the door?"

Lyra was safe at school. At least, I hoped so. There was nothing I could do from the tower tonight. The sooner this job was over, the sooner I could see her again. I set the knife back on the dresser, but still within easy reach, and moved to the door. I undid the lock and opened the door to find a brunette smiling on the other side. The angel was dressed in a slinky gold number; her hair hung past her shoulders in soft waves. Celeste exuded confidence, class, and luxury. She seemed a perfect match to the dark, broody, and smoldering archangel I'd met so far, except her wings were ivory gilded in gold. A pang of jealousy hit me. To have wings and status, Celeste was blessed indeed.

"What do you know about Lyra?" I asked. She smiled, her brilliant white teeth glistening in the dim light.

"Your sister is a darling. Underfed and skittish, but already looking forward to settling in at school. Her roommate is a decent gal; quiet, scholarly, and shares a mutual love of plants," Celeste said. "Lyra's worried about you but glad to hear that you're safe in the tower. You look great, by the way. Half the angels at The Feather won't know whether to admire you or disapprove. I like how you paired the dress. Not my first choice, but I'm not the one wearing it. You make it shine. Do you need any help with hair, makeup, or your cutlery?" she asked with an amused glance at the knife resting on top of the dresser.

"It was an insurance policy. A woman can't be too careful," I responded, as I picked up the plastic key card from beside the knife.

"A kitchen knife works in a pinch against humans. Come see me tomorrow—Icarus or I have a few better suited items you can keep with you at all times, if you wish. An ordinary chef's knife won't do much against an angel or demon except to piss it off. Speaking of Icarus, he made this band for you. If you don't care for the look, you can get another made," Celeste explained, offering me the gold band. I took it from her reluctantly. It was a solid band with delicate feathers engraved around it except for a line of text—*Spes, Veritas, Lux.*

"I'm not versed in Arcadian. What does it say?" I

inquired, and Celeste smiled with a warmth that lit her dark eyes.

"It's not Arcadian. It's Latin for hope, truth, and light. Icarus was a good friend of your father. He inscribed the bracelet with your father's motto. Ramiel believed in hope and truth above all else and that they would light the path to salvation even during the darkest of times," Celeste said. I slipped the bracelet over my wrist; it was a snug fit but comfortable. The metal was warm against my skin where Kassian had clasped cool handcuffs not even twenty-four hours earlier.

Like father, like daughter.

"Not that it did him much good," I responded. "He lied to you all." Celeste frowned.

"No, he didn't. He protected the lights of his life—his girls. There were a few of us he trusted with his secrets. A few of us did everything we could to protect him and give his girls the freedom he wanted for you. You and your sister are the first halflings of an archangel, you know. Ramiel did everything he could so you would have a childhood with your mother, may she rest in peace. Come on, we're late," Celeste said before she turned and left the room.

I felt frozen as I trailed my fingers over the engraving on the band. *Spes, Veritas, Lux*—hope, truth, and light were more than his motto. They were the angel gifts we had inherited from him. Hopefully, they would be enough to keep me out of the Pit and the door to hell sealed shut.

The walk to the elevator was short, the descent to the bar was even shorter, except Celeste reached out and pushed the emergency stop button. The elevator halted jarringly. I reached out to the metal walls to catch myself before I fell.

"Everyone you meet tonight is a potential enemy except for Kassian, Icarus, and I. Be careful. Some of the clientele here are angels that work for Kassian, some are visitors from other cities, and there is always a demon liaison or two lurking around. Many of the people here will welcome you, some will despise you, and to others, you'll be a mere curiosity," Celeste said casually, clearly well versed in the comings and goings of the tower.

"Why did my father trust you?" I asked, as Celeste moved to push the button.

"He trusted Icarus, but only Ramiel could answer that question," Celeste said softly. The grimace on her face and pain in her eyes were enough to know she grieved a loss of her own. I didn't need to know. I didn't want to know. She was an ally and kind to Lyra —*that's* all I needed to know.

"Understood," I responded. She nodded and pushed the elevator button. It moved smoothly once again until it came to a gentle stop, and the doors opened.

"I forgot to ask. Do you have any experience bartending?" Celeste asked.

"Not really," I admitted as I willed my hands not to fidget. Bars tended to be overwhelming for me; lies fell from drunken lips as easily as deep sunken secrets. For a half-angel with barely any control over my gift, my single previous attempt at working in a bar was utter torture. I barely lasted the night. Celeste frowned as she sensed my hesitation.

"Waiting tables?" she asked hopefully.

"Yes," I readily responded. Waiting tables was much

easier to manage. Celeste smiled and nodded in acceptance.

"Stick to what you know and the rest will come. The bartenders have been instructed to help you," she assured me and stepped forward into a display of class, luxury, and rustic sophistication I'd never associate with the bars of East Haven.

In East Haven, you'd find pool tables, clouds of smoke, and more conflict than empty glasses. Here, though, people, angels, and demons mingled with ease. It was well-lit but soft, giving warmth to the space. Floor-to-ceiling glass windows offering a view of the city were flanked by ivory curtains. The patrons at the leather booths and industrial-style wooden tables could pull the curtains closed if they preferred. I never would, though. The city sparkled in the growing night. Buildings and streets below glittered like diamonds on display against the velvet night sky. I could hear soft jazz music playing over a sound system, adding to the hum of the restaurant, even though a piano sat just outside of the elevators, marking a lobby of sorts. Lyra would have been delighted to run her fingers along the keys. Instead, a familiar angel sat on the bench, dressed all in black, with his burgundy wings on display behind him.

Kassian sat there, looking down at his phone, texting frantically. I heard the soft ding of a cell phone chime from beside me. Celeste's. His head swung up at the noise. The look of surprise and pleasure on his face before he schooled his features into neutrality was all the confirmation I needed that I'd made the right wardrobe choice. He approved, if the heat in that look was anything to go by. He rose from the piano bench swiftly and walked toward me.

"There you two are. I was wondering if you decided not to come," Kassian teased, even though he seemed relieved, which struck me as odd. He hadn't really given me a choice to say no; a deal was a deal, but maybe he didn't see it that way. Celeste laughed, the sound joyful and free.

"Only you skip your first day on the job," Celeste taunted.

"Never going to let me live that down, are you?" Kassian laughed, sounding warm and sexy. "Nora, you look divine," Kassian said with a smile. "Thank you for showing her the way, Celeste."

"My pleasure. I'll be back later. I need to check in with a few folks," Celeste said with a smile and wave before sauntering off toward the back of the restaurant.

"Celeste was helpful, I hope?" Kassian asked.

"She's a talker," I mentioned quietly. Kassian snickered as he attempted to control his laughter.

"She always is. It's one thing I love about her. She doesn't take no for an answer and says it how it is," Kassian nodded while grinning. Nothing was wrong with his statement, but it still irritated me. I smiled regardless.

"A handy woman to have at your side," I admitted. Kassian's smile grew, as I wanted nothing more than for the conversation to change to something other than the brunette angel that held his favor.

"Not tonight, at least. Come along, little angel. There are some people I want you to meet," Kassian said. "Welcome to The Feather, where angels can be a bit more human."

"Cute name," I responded. "Is there The Pool, The Laundry Mat, and The Divine Doggie Groomer?"

"All right, all right. I didn't say it was the most creative of names, but it is mine. You can at least pretend you like it," Kassian said with a laugh.

"It has its charm," I responded, and tucked my arm around his. If he wanted arm candy tonight, I might as well start now. He put his warm hand over mine and held it there as he began a quick tour of the restaurant and bar.

The wait staff was dressed to impress in black and ivory outfits. The patrons already seated were all relaxed. Many had their suit jackets and blazers removed, hanging on hooks or the back of their chairs. Very few still had ties on. Mostly, all the men looked similar to Mercer in business attire and even hairstyle, as if they all saw the same barber, except for their wings. So far, I hadn't seen a set of wings that matched another exactly. It was as if each set of wings was unique to the angel.

It was clear not everyone was an angel. One man was obviously part demon based on the horns curving from his wavy hair. The demon's red eyes tracked our approach. Across from him sat an angel with wings the darkest shade of emerald I had ever seen. It was even more startling when I felt a darkness beckon, as if a shadow was trying to invade my mind.

Hello, angel. I was wondering when Kass would let you come out to play. The voice purred into my mind. The attractive archangel with dark emerald iridescent wings winked at me before sipping at the tumbler in his hand. *Welcome to The Feather, halfling.*

CHAPTER 9

The angel looked away after acknowledging me, but the demon across from him had no such reservations. The demon's red eyes glowed faintly as he grinned at me like I was a feast he had been waiting for.

"Carakus, Silas—any news?" Kassian asked them calmly.

"Something tells me she's not on the menu," the demon murmured.

I laughed despite the unnatural pull I felt toward the demon until Kassian tightened his grip on my arm. A pulse of heat throbbed from beneath his hand onto my arm, warm and stinging, pulling my attention away from the demon.

"No, definitely not. You know the rules, Carakus. If you need to satisfy your needs with something other than alcohol or causal fare, you'll have to find your meal elsewhere. The Feather doesn't offer those options here," Kassian said stiffly in warning.

"Pity. That's a rare rose you have there, Viscount.

You best keep her locked in this tower as long as you can before someone else plucks her," Carakus growled. "Otherwise, I have no news to report."

"So, this must be the angel halfling turning East Haven on its head," the angel with emerald wings said, his voice the same malty timber as the voice that caressed my mind. His hair was styled back, no horns in sight, but his brown eyes were nearly black. He smirked, and I thought I saw fangs, but it was gone in a flash, hidden beneath stern amused lips and a well-groomed beard. "It's nice not to be the source of scandal for once."

"You're always the source of scandal, Silas. You don't know how *not* to be," Kassian responded lightly. Silas slapped his hand on the table and raised his glass in Kassian's direction.

"Right you are, brother," Silas agreed.

"Oh, is this the lost angel you found hiding in the East End? I should have known," Carakus grumbled.

"Gentlemen, this is Miss Nora Evans, daughter of Ramiel," Kassian spoke.

I waved at the two predators. One clearly demon, the other not quite an angel if those were truly fangs I saw. Maybe Lyra and I weren't the only angel halflings in this city, but I had never heard of an angel-demon halfling.

"Carakus, tell Kass what you told me," Silas ushered, waving his hand at the demon before taking a long drink of the whiskey in front of him. Carakus gave Silas a side-eye and grunted.

"Demons are divided. For every lead we have, there are five opposing statements. If demons are mobilizing, it's a small sect that is moving against angels in a very coordinated manner," Carakus said. "We're not sure if demons are involved at all."

The lie smelled like an open jar of honey. It even sounded false to my ears, like a chord plucked wrong. The only problem was I had no way to tell Kassian without showing my talent to the two men in front of me. I reached out and took Silas's glass from him; I took a large drink, finishing what I hoped was his whiskey for him. He tilted his head at me, amused, and smirked.

What are you up to, girl? Silas purred in my mind.

The invasion into my mind almost caused me to drop the glass.

"It looked too tempting not to try. I'll get you another. Sounds like you boys will be here a while. Demons are always involved, same as angels," I said coyly before disengaging my arm from Kassian's. I kissed him on the cheek, unhurriedly trailing my hand along his arm before I sashayed my way slowly in the bar's direction with Silas's empty glass in my hand. I could still barely hear their conversation continue on without me.

"She's a wild card, that one," Silas said appreciatively.

"East Enders always are. I'm serious, Kassian—keep that one locked in this tower as long as she'll let you. We know you were within your rights to send Maximus back to the Pit at that foolhardy auction, but it upset many that she slipped through our fingers. I suspect the Bookie of East End had a public auction in the hopes you'd stop it. He could have retired if he'd sold her privately to our sector. Is it true she has a sister?" I heard the red-eyed demon ask. I forced myself to trust Kassian and not slow my steps to listen to the rest of the conversation. Kassian was an entrepreneur, not a monster. He wouldn't, couldn't, put my sister at risk. Would he?

"Come on now, Carakus, I've never known you to be so enamored with a woman. She's right though, demons have to be involved. How can there—" the rest of Kassian's sentence was lost in the lounge's noise. I quickly made my way to the bar and set the tumbler down on the polished wood.

"What are you drinking, lass?" the bartender asked. No wings. No demon eyes. Could she be human?

"Another round of whatever whiskey this was," I answered. The bartender laughed as she took the glass.

"Who was drinking it?" she quizzed. I pointed at the table behind me where the three men still sat. I could no longer hear the conversation, but I knew it would continue.

"Silas," I responded, and her brown eyes widened. She placed whiskey cubes into two new tumblers and set an expensive bottle on the bar.

"Are you Nora?" she inquired.

"Yes," I said, surprised. The bartender nodded with a smile before wiping her hands on a dry cloth and offered her hand out to shake mine.

"Celeste said you might come by to help man the bar. My name's Violet. Why don't you drop those off and come back when you can? Kassian and Silas drink the same. The demon doesn't drink here and will be gone soon," Violet explained.

With glasses in one hand and whiskey in the other, I made my way back to Kassian and the others. After setting the glasses on the table, I poured a tall drink for the two angels that watched me closely. Kassian smiled and winked at me while Silas retrieved his drink.

"I'll be around if you boys need me," I said and walked away, taking the whiskey bottle with me. If they needed a refill, they'd have to come and get it. I wasn't ready to chance Kassian under the influence.

How much alcohol would it take to put an angel under the table? Question for another night.

"Thanks, love," Kassian purred.

I turned back to see him smirk and wink at me before sipping at the whiskey and turning back to his conversation with Carakus and Silas. Refusing to label the feeling bubbling up within me, I turned back for the bar, determined to make myself useful as more than his arm candy tonight.

The night grew long, and the requests didn't end. Violet made more complicated concoctions, leaving the simpler orders and clean-up to me. The air around me was thick with lies as patrons tried to sweet talk their companions and con businessmen. They might be angels, but there were no saints among them, except maybe Violet. I still hadn't figured out if she was an angel or not. I noticed a lull while I wiped down the bar for the hundredth time when Violet approached me.

"Hey, girl, grab a seat and take a break. Here, I think you'll like this," Violet said, holding out a tall glass of something bubbly with cherries mixed in.

"What is it?" I asked, taking the cool glass from her.

"Lemon-lime soda with cherries and extra lime. No alcohol," Violet said sincerely, no hint of a lie.

"We don't drink on the job if we can help it, unless we're taste-testing something new. Isn't that right, Kass?" Violet said teasingly, her voice bright and pleased. I was surprised by how casual she was with his name.

"Couldn't agree more. How are you holding up, little angel?" Kassian asked as he came up beside me. He reached out with one hand and stroked my arm lazily with soft fingers. I sat at the bar, taking a long drink of the soda as he sat next to me. Violet was right. It was refreshing and bright, a perfect mix of sweet and tart.

"I'm holding my own. How about you, sir?" I responded with a smile. He shifted his weight to lean closer to me as he grinned.

"Just fine," Kassian said, just as two angels approached. The woman I recognized—Celeste. The man, I did not, but he was gorgeous. His brilliant white and gold wings glowed dimly against his bronze skin. Unlike the rest of the men I had met tonight, he wasn't in a suit. He was dressed casually in designer jeans and a button-down shirt.

"Celeste, Icarus, so glad you could join us. Icarus, this is Nora. Nora, this is Icarus," Kassian said. Icarus smiled and nodded at me in greeting.

"Hello, Nora. You've grown since I saw you last. It's been nearly fourteen years. Is the bracelet to your satisfaction?" Icarus asked, his accent lilting and musical. I smiled. I had the faintest memory of him from long ago. He had visited my father at home once, just before Lyra was born.

"You came to our home once. You brought a music box for my mother," I said. A box my mother used to coax Lyra to sleep as a newborn. Lyra adored it almost as much as her harp. Icarus smiled and nodded in acknowledgement. "The bracelet is beautiful. It'll just take a bit of time to get used to."

"May I?" Icarus asked as he reached toward the band on my wrist. I offered my wrist to him. He didn't remove the band. Instead, he held it gently in his hands without touching my skin before running his thumbs across it. The metal grew warm for a brief second, then shifted and molded beneath his fingers to fit my wrist more comfortably, like a well-worn watch.

"How?" I asked as Kassian and Celeste smiled at us. Icarus looked amused and proud for a moment.

"My gift is invention and manipulation of objects," Icarus explained as he released my wrist.

"Oh, I'd say it's a bit more than that," Kassian interjected. Icarus scoffed and ignored him.

"Thank you for adjusting the bracelet," I responded.

"Of course. Anything for a daughter of Ramiel," Icarus responded. "Speaking of which, I should get back to the shop; I was in the middle of a project. I'm almost done, but Celeste insisted I come."

"You know I'd do anything to get you to leave your workshop for an hour. I'll walk back with you, love," Celeste offered, and Icarus kissed her on the cheek. I looked at Kassian, but he had no reaction to the interaction.

"Don't be a stranger, Nora," Celeste said. "Come see me tomorrow about the trinket we discussed. Icarus and I should have something for you by then."

Then the two angels walked away, hand in hand. It was then I noticed their wings were exactly the same pattern, but they were a different size. Celeste's were smaller than Icarus's, as if their wings were suited to their size but otherwise mirror images.

"What are you thinking, little angel?" Kassian asked as he sipped from my drink. I turned to him. He looked more relaxed now compared to the tension radiating from him when I first stepped off the elevator.

"Are they related? Their wings match," I asked.

"When angels ascend, they develop wings. When two angels are soul mates, their wings are identical. Celeste and Icarus—they're soulmates," Kassian explained.

"I thought you and Celeste—" I stopped as Kassian chuckled and set my glass back down in front of me.

"By Arcadia, no!" Kassian said, aghast. "She's my cousin. She's like a sister to me. Icarus was visiting me when Celeste ascended because he was near. The moment her wings revealed themselves, they knew what it meant. They've been nearly inseparable since. They're a powerful couple. All mated angels are." A chuckle sounded next to me.

"Easy there, Kassian. You'll scare her off with your talk of mates," Silas said. "You don't have to worry about mates, wild one."

"Oh yeah, and why is that?" I questioned before I gave Silas a disgruntled look and downed the rest of my drink. Silas grinned knowingly as he looked at me with unwavering eye contact.

"Human-halflings don't ascend. You won't get wings; therefore, no mate. You can have all the fun you want, with whoever you want," Silas suggested. If I didn't know better, I thought I heard a soft grumble from Kassian behind me.

"I have plenty of fun," I said quietly. Silas's smile only grew in response.

"Oh, is that true?" Silas teased in a light tone before he leaned in close, his lips almost brushing my ear. "That's not what the shadows tell me."

"Shadows don't talk," I said, and frowned at the confusing halfling.

"They talk a lot, especially the ones in your head

that hide all your secrets. You should let loose more and have some fun. We only live once, you know," Silas chided.

"I'm aware and I don't need a halfling to give me permission," I snapped back. His eyes smoldered.

Careful, girl. This isn't East End. Humans are easy to con. I am not, Silas growled into my mind in warning as his index finger circled the top of my glass before he put it up to his mouth.

"Mmm, sweet and tart, with a hint of a bite. Just like you," Silas purred out loud before winking at me.

"Enough, Silas," Kassian growled as he rose from his seat to stand beside me. He draped his arm across my shoulder.

"When you've had your fun with Kassian, come find me. I'll play with you, halfling. You can do anything you want; you won't need my permission. I'm not one for rules anyway," Silas admitted with a sideways glance at Kassian and a devious smirk. "Your move, Kass. The game's just begun." Silas pulled a coin from his pocket and tossed it at Kassian. Kassian plucked it from the air before he cursed and pocketed what appeared to be an elaborate poker piece. "Violet, a bottle to go! I think I'm done at The Feather tonight."

Stay close to Kass, don't get sloppy. He'll keep you safe. Silas's voice echoed in my mind as he walked away. *There are ears listening, and eyes watching, so make it look real. Or at least have some fun. If you're in trouble, call me. We halflings have to stick together... even if you're half-human.*

"Who exactly is Silas?" I asked as I put my empty glass on the bar-top. "What's with the coin?"

"Silas's gifts allow him to manage the Pit, act as a demon liaison, be a general pain in my ass most days, and my best friend," Kassian responded. "The coin is a game we've been playing for years."

"What kind of game?" I asked suspiciously.

"That would be telling. Let's just say he's much better at it because most rules don't apply to him," Kassian hinted.

"Hmm, he seems nice," I offered. Kassian merely snickered in response before he leaned close. "The other demon you two were talking to, not so much. He lied to you about the demons' involvement. At least Silas is honest, if a bit devious."

"Little angel, you have no idea," Kassian said before kissing me on the cheek. "Come talk to me about what you heard and sensed."

CHAPTER 10

Before the night was through, Kassian and I sat in a corner booth close together like a pair of lovebirds. Instead of whispering sweet nothings into my ear as we people-watched, he told me all about his patrons—-who was who, what they did, their skill sets, and who to avoid if Kassian wasn't around. Violet kept the drinks coming but didn't say a word. Neither of us ordered anything more potent than soda water.

It was weird being this close to him, his breath caressing my ear. His arm across my shoulder, his fingers absentmindedly drawing patterns on my sleeve. It was distracting, sexy, and downright confusing. I couldn't tell if it was part of the ruse with him or simply casual attention. Regardless, it was working. More than one angel took notice of our closeness. Some came over to introduce themselves; others smirked and walked on.

"Do you normally shower women with this much attention at The Feather?" I asked as I stirred the melting ice around in my drink with the cocktail straw.

"Normally, I don't bring my women to The Feather. I rarely mix business and pleasure. The patrons know it, so you're going to be a novelty at first, but they'll get used to it. Better they get used to you like this than as the rebel halfling," Kassian said. "By morning, they won't be talking about your actions in East Haven, only how you seem to have ensnared me."

"Like they would believe that you, the archangel in charge of all of New Haven, and me, a nobody from the shadows, could ever be something," I scoffed. Kassian brought his hand up beneath my chin, his fingers gently forcing me to look up at him. His eyes smoldered with challenge.

"Maybe you should help me make them believe it, little angel," Kassian challenged. "You are far from nobody to me."

The edges of Kassian's lips turned up in a smile, the challenge enticing but the smile even more so. He might be a bit of a prick and an archangel to boot, but Kassian was an attractive man. It was no hardship to lean forward and kiss him as my body hummed with anticipation. His hand wrapped firmly around my hair and neck, and using his hold to bring me closer, his lips captured mine. He tasted of citrus, soda water, and whiskey. His free hand wrapped around my waist and tugged me onto his lap as I lost myself to the kiss. The din of The Feather faded as I refused to submit under his kiss and held my own. He nipped at my lower lip. Two could play at that game. I pulled his lower lip into my mouth with a gentle tug. It was a mistake, as his tongue invaded my mouth.

A loud cough sounded beside the table, startling

me. Kassian didn't pull away. He merely tightened his hold on my waist. This was the archangel in charge, and he would not be corralled by a mere cough.

"Viscount Kassian, hate to interrupt," the voice sneered. I recognized it.

Mercer.

Kassian stopped and eased away from me with a frustrated sigh, as if he were truly irritated at the interruption. To be honest, I was a bit as well, but also thankful. The kiss was escalating outside the realm of fake and all for show, to a bit... more. I was thoroughly enjoying it, my heartbeat still raced and my lips still tingled from the kissing.

"Kassian, you're walking a fine line."

"Look at her. She's breathtaking. I had to indulge in a bite or two. Any man would, even you," Kassian suggested as he kissed me again. Mercer grunted in disapproval, his mouth pinched as he turned away from the affectionate display.

"Some men, maybe," he sneered. Kassian's easy demeanor shifted from hot to icy as he turned toward the other angel.

"What is it, Mercer?" Kassian asked, annoyed.

"Parliament has called a meeting. We've been summoned to the House of Lords," Mercer responded. "Best to put your pet away and get there now."

"I'll decide what's best. Message delivered. I'll see you there," Kassian said. Mercer frowned disapprovingly at me.

"Remember what I said, girl. You have potential, but only if you make the right choices," Mercer said before turning to leave.

"He's a bitter man," I responded.

THE ARCHANGEL'S DEAL

"My uncle is complicated. He lost a lot during the war. It changed him," Kassian responded.

"Uncle?" I asked.

"Celeste and Mercer are the last of my family. Mercer lost his wife in the wars. Celeste and I lost our parents," Kassian explained.

"That's why you put up with him?" I questioned. Kassian merely laughed.

"No, I put up with him because he's a shrewd businessman and a strong ally to have when you're trying to run a city. You may not think much of the city, but eventually, I mean to pull East Haven out of the shadows... if it'll let me," Kassian said.

"What do you mean?" I asked.

"In a way, East Haven is the last battleground between angels and demons in this city. Restorative justice, charity, and rehabilitative community efforts do little while humans welcome demons, and their deals, with open arms. Darkness begets darkness. At least we've put a stop to selling firstborn children. The rest will come with time as long as we're successful in our endeavors, little angel," Kassian said.

I knew about the charity and rehabilitative attempts he spoke of. They were usually mocked and avoided by the prideful. My mother went to a clinic every week until they told her there was nothing more they could do. She didn't last much longer after that. There were too few supplies to go around for everyone in need. I had stood in more than one soup kitchen line only for the doors to shutter before I saw a single morsel. Eventually, you stop trying to do things the right way and do whatever it takes to survive. I'd compromised my morals more than once to make sure food was on the table for Lyra. I'd do it again if I had to.

"Nora?" Kassian asked, concern in his tone.

"Hmm?"

"I asked if you wanted to go to the House of Lords with me. If you're not up for it, you don't have to come. I can take you back to the penthouse," Kassian offered.

"Go to the House of Lords as a visitor and not as a person of interest?" I asked, pretending to be falsely taken aback. Kassian grinned.

"You'll always be a person of interest, but as a visitor, yes," Kassian responded, trying not to laugh.

"It could be fun," I demurred.

"Hopefully not," Kassian said. "Follow me."

He helped me out of the booth. Most of The Feather had emptied after Mercer's visit. I wondered if that meant most of the patrons had been summoned as well. We walked past the bar on the way to the elevator.

"Good night, Violet, lock up for me, please."

"Will do, Kass. Good night," Violet responded before turning back to the bar-top she was cleaning for the hundredth time. The elevator doors opened, and he ushered me inside. It began its ascent but didn't stop at the penthouse like I expected. It continued to the roof.

"The roof?" I questioned, but then the doors slid open to show a rooftop getaway. I expected concrete and metal; instead, I was greeted with a well-lit garden oasis with marked landing pads for incoming angels high above the din of the city. A night breeze caused chimes to tinkle and ring. The garden had its charm, with chaises and lounge chairs, but the view was beyond measure.

Across the city, I could see that more rooftops than not had been converted to secret oases for angels. To the north, the city glowed the brightest and grew darker to the East and West Ends. Across the city, you could see the silhouettes of angels as they took flight, all of them headed in a similar direction—north, to the House of Lords.

"I sometimes forget what it must be like for others not to see this," Kassian said softly. "Or to see it for the first time."

"Definitely not what I would have imagined from the street," I responded. I dreamed of seeing the city from heights like this for years, but my imagination never did it justice.

"It gets better," Kassian promised.

"I doubt that." I laughed and turned to Kassian. He smiled, his massive burgundy wings appearing behind him. The light of the night reflected gently off the golden edges, giving his wings the illusion that they glowed. He offered me his hand.

"Fly with me?" Kassian asked. My heart squeezed with painful hope. To fly was all I had ever wanted. I'd never imagined this was how my first time would be.

"Yes," I responded, and took his hand. He squeezed my hand reassuringly before dropping it. He glamoured his wings away, shrugged out of his jacket, then formed his wings again.

"You'll need this. It's a brisk night," Kassian said, handing me his blazer. I slipped into the oversized garment. Once the jacket settled against my shoulders, he stepped forward, swooped low, and scooped me up into his arms. Clutching me close to his chest, he stepped closer to the edge of the roof where the railing had been removed.

"Trust me?" Kassian asked.

"No," I responded, as I slipped my arms around his neck and clenched my hands together. He laughed.

"Hold on, little angel," was the only warning he gave before we were falling. I closed my eyes against our pending death.

Air whooshed past. His arms clutched me tight. Then suddenly, everything shifted, and instead of free-falling to the cement below, we were soaring down the avenue and back up into the sky. I felt the muscles along his shoulders, back, and chest working to beat his wings and propel us higher into the cool night air.

"Open your eyes, Nora. You'll want to see this," Kassian said. He was right. I snapped my eyes open.

Above us, clouds and stars mingled together in a glittering patchwork. Below, the city backed a soft dim glow on the horizon. Ahead of us, on the largest hill at the edge of the northern forest, sat an old colonial relic of a mansion. Its white walls glowed in the darkness, a beacon, a fortress.

The House of Lords.

CHAPTER 11

The last time I was here was for my father's mockery of a trial. They sent a blacked-out town car for us when the labor and delivery doctor discharged my mother. My father wasn't even allowed to be present when they dragged my mother, baby sister, and me before Parliament as proof of his indiscretions. A cold group of angels had frowned down on us from their perches.

After questioning my mother's relationship, an angel approached my sister and me. The black-haired angel with purple wings, dressed in a white suit, at least smiled at me. She showed me a picture of my father, asking me who he was. I refused to say a word, but I didn't need to. My likeness to him was clear, and my mother's testimony was enough to imprison a regular angel. Still, they couldn't imprison an archangel on a human's word alone. After I refused to speak, the same angel placed her hand on my head without even a question of consent. For a moment, my skin glowed bright, painlessly. The angel frowned and looked remorseful, but then took the same actions with my sister in my mother's arms, receiving the same reaction. Then she finally moved on to my mother, but no light was shown this time. Angel, angel, human. All the proof they needed to condemn Ramiel with only the touch of a hand.

At least in the darkness of night, the House of Lords didn't look as menacing as it did back then. The flight was calm, almost tranquil. The beat of Kassian's wings and the heat from his body nearly lulled me to sleep. As Kassian flew closer, he avoided the gates and sentinels that were merely the first line of defense for the fortress within. He landed us directly on an open balcony on the second floor of the well-lit mansion.

"I'm surprised you didn't scream. Did you keep your eyes closed the entire time?" Kassian asked. He looked windswept, and I suspected I did as well. He stretched his massive wings wide for a moment. He flapped them once, then made them disappear.

"No, only at the beginning. I've always wanted to fly. I wanted to go to the flight academy, but I couldn't find one to accept me," I admitted hesitantly. Most schools had rejected my application because of my parentage. The rest I couldn't afford, and no one wanted to give scholarships to halflings of branded traitors.

"You want to be a pilot, to fly?" Kassian asked as he stared at me.

"Yes," I admitted with a shrug, expecting to be scoffed at. My mother and sister had believed in me. Only my mother and sister seemed to understand how I felt called to the skies. No one else ever did. I waited for him to laugh at me as so many had before. Instead, Kassian genuinely smiled.

"You'll have to earn your wings on your own, but if you're open to the idea, Icarus or I might be able to help you find a school that won't ask too many questions," Kassian responded, seeing straight through to the issue.

"Thank you," I breathed, trying not to let hope rise in my chest. I had given up on that dream.

"Do you always fall when you fly?" I asked. Kassian laughed before he ducked his head close to mine for a quick, soft kiss. Earlier was a competition. This was something else—something gentle and sweet. His lips were cool and soft against mine, and my lips tingled from the touch. He smelled of the night air; it was calming and different from the smell of the streets and pollution I was used to in the city. I wanted to bottle the scent and keep it with me. He pulled away slowly and brushed my hair away from my face with a soft caress.

"I prefer soaring to generate lift over using my wings to create it. Less effort," Kassian explained.

"Like a bird," I teased. The corners of his mouth turned up into a smile.

"Don't let anyone else hear you saying that, little angel. They may take offense." He chuckled. "Come on, we should move before someone else tries to land."

Kassian didn't say more. He simply turned and strode into the foreboding structure. While the building didn't seem as big as it had a lifetime ago, it was still as frigid. I followed Kassian through the long, harsh hallway. Luxurious carpets muffled our footsteps, and large tapestries depicting warrior angels and the Arcadian Wars covered the walls. The images always showed angels as victors over demons, the weeping masses of humans always shoved into the background, if they were even shown at all. The hallway we walked through led to a large marble staircase. It was grand, but it did not compare to the painting that adorned the ceiling above it. I hadn't noticed it last time I was at this forbidding palace, likely because I was too busy staring at my feet, wishing they could take me anywhere else.

The painting was so captivating that I stumbled on the stairs. Kassian barely kept me from falling as he gripped my arm. Pictured above us was the entire Arcadian War, summarized in a single image. Humans cried out. Angels and demons warred. In the middle of it all, five angels glowed in front of a rather old-fashioned gate that resembled the one at the Pit. The five angels wore crowns, their wings displayed, their faces fierce with determination. Yet that wasn't what caused me to stumble on the first step up the staircase. The fifth angel was unmistakable—blond hair and green eyes blazing. His vibrant emerald wings edged in silver matched the crown on his head—Ramiel, my father.

"Nora?" Kassian said as I continued to stare up at the ceiling.

"He was one of the angels that sealed the gate?" I asked. Kassian swung his head up to look at the painting, and his mouth became a terse line.

"He was," Kassian responded. "And the youngest of the five that succeeded."

"Succeeded?"

"We lost more than a few archangels trying to close the gate. What you won't hear from most these days is that if it weren't for Ramiel, it likely wouldn't have been successful at all. Your father saved many lives that day," Kassian explained. "We can talk more about this later. I need to get inside. Do you want to stay out here?"

"No." I shook my head. "I'll go in with you."

"I'll need my blazer back for a bit. I'll return it for the flight back to the tower," Kassian promised. I shrugged out of the blazer and handed it to him. He pulled it on quickly and took the stairs two at a time. I followed behind as fast as I could, though I felt pulled to inspect the painting above us more closely.

At the top of the stairs, two broad-shouldered angels in suits guarded the double doors. They acknowledged Kassian with a nod, then looked at me with curiosity.

"Who's the woman?" the taller angel asked.

"She is my guest tonight," Kassian explained.

"Make sure she keeps quiet," one burly guard responded as he opened the doors to let us in. He sent a pointed look my way in warning. "There should be seats at the back you can take."

"Of course," Kassian responded. He took my hand and led me through the doors.

Row upon row of wooden benches were lined up in a semicircle, all facing a raised panel of nine archangels. A shiver echoed down my spine and along my skin; it was a mistake coming here. This was no place for a halfling, a reject, an abomination to their way of life.

I was grateful when Kassian released my hand and gestured to an empty seat in the last row closest to the door. The seat was the furthest I could get away from the collection of angels seated at the front of the room as they talked amongst themselves. I had barely sat on the hard wooden bench before Kassian turned and strode to the front of the room to sit in the first row beside a scowling Mercer.

From his posture and how Mercer bent to whisper in Kassian's ear, I suspected he was expressing his disapproval over my presence. The pound of a gavel brought my attention back up to the panel. The oldest looking angel banged his gavel twice more, and silence reigned throughout the room.

"The humans have not been called to this meeting for security reasons. Now that all regents are accounted for, let us begin," the angel announced, his voice a husky rasp that echoed across the room. He was seated in the center of the table of elevated angels, a mallet rested on the table beside him. He appeared to be the angel in charge.

It was then I realized that every seat in the first three rows was full of angels. Kassian had been the last one to sit. The rows behind them were empty. Most of the angels looked windswept and rushed from their dinners and beds. Yet, they had been waiting for Kassian. He knew they would be, but he still took the time to bring me and even kiss me on the balcony. My lips were still tingling from those crushing kisses.

"We are here this evening because another legacy has been attacked and a second angel has gone missing just this night. It has come to our attention that this is not an isolated incident. This is happening across all cities and regions that have a demon presence. Somehow, it appears the demons have found a way to circumvent the Arcadian Treaty and the angel-bond," the old angel stated. "Viscount Kassian Oriel of New Haven, how many angels have you lost to this scourge? Do you have any leads?"

Kassian rose from his seat, his wings flaring to life as he stepped forward.

"Duke Manuel, seven angels from New Haven have been impacted, two have lost their lives, and another is still missing. We do not have any leads or suspects at this time," Kassian answered. The old archangel frowned from his perch and grunted.

"Why did you not mention this to the House?" Duke Manuel asked.

"I was hoping to discover the culprit within the city before panic ensued or spooking them into hiding," Kassian explained. "We are working closely with our human counterparts and demon liaisons."

Murmuring and unrest rose in the room as many started quiet side conversations. The old archangel banged his gavel three times before turning to the angel beside him and whispering to her. The pair continued their hushed conversation as silence fell.

"Baron Mercer, step forward. What do you have to say about recent events in New Haven?" the female angel spoke up. Mercer rose swiftly and stood beside Kassian without a second look at him.

"Duchess Yesenia, it is hard times when angels are not safe in their own homes. The Viscount and I are working to ensure the safety of all," Mercer affirmed.

"Do you think we should be working with humans and demons at this time? Have humans or demons suffered any losses?" the angel asked, smiling softly down at Mercer.

"It is not my place to disagree with my Viscount. As far as I am aware, only angels have been affected by this strife," Mercer responded. Kassian's back stiffened in response, his fists clenched.

"Do you think humans are working with demons?" the Duke asked.

"I can't say for sure. There is very little love between angels and humans. The demons thrive off humans in the city despite our attempts to protect them from the darkness," Mercer said.

"Are the humans of New Haven a lost cause?" the Duchess asked.

"No," Kassian responded.

"Possibly," Mercer said candidly.

"What is this rumor of an angel being sold on the streets of New Haven?" the Duchess asked.

It was definitely a mistake coming here tonight.

"I can answer that, Duchess," Kassian spoke up. "It was a misunderstanding that allowed us to address an underlying issue in New Haven. It was not malicious in any way, nor related to the recent attacks and missing angels."

"So the angel being sold was not one of our missing angels? Not a legacy angel?" Duchess Yesenia asked.

"No, she was not a missing angel," Kassian responded firmly. "Simply in the wrong place at the wrong time."

"Then why was this angel not brought before us?" Duke Manuel asked. "Baron Mercer, what do you know of this?"

"I can only assume you are referring to a halfling that Viscount Kassian rescued from unfortunate circumstances. She is not a pure-blooded angel, but she is now in the Viscount's care. I suspect he did not want to bother you with a trivial halfling given the current circumstances," Mercer suggested lightly.

"There are only so many halflings in New Haven. Was the halfling a legacy?" the Duchess asked knowingly. Kassian remained silent as Mercer looked at him, then back at the angel above him.

"Yes, Duchess, the eldest daughter of Ramiel," Mercer said before looking at Kassian again and sighed. "In fact, she's here tonight."

"Really? Then pray tell, where is she?" the Duchess said with an excited laugh. Mercer turned around, looked at me, and grinned. He raised his hand and pointed at me. Everyone turned to look. He curled his finger, beckoning me forward. I scowled at Mercer, my ire rising. I was not a child to be beckoned, though I was likely the youngest person in the room and a child by some angels' standards.

"Come here, Nora," Mercer ordered aloud, his voice tense and stern. Kassian caught my eye and nodded stiffly, the only additional encouragement I needed. I rose from the bench and slowly walked to the front of the room. Nine sets of eyes looked down on me from above as the rest of the room stared at me.

"You are Nora of Ramiel, one of the fifth?" the Duchess asked, her voice calm and kind.

"I am Nora Evans, daughter of the Archangel Ramiel and Sarah Evans, Duchess," I answered, looking straight at the angel without regret. I knew where I came from. I was proud of my parents, even if the rest of the angels had scoffed at their love. Their love did not recognize labels and rules. My parents had loved true to their hearts.

"Were you forced into being sold?" the Duchess asked.

"It was a misunderstanding. Before I could leave, the man I trusted used the angel-bond to keep me compliant," I responded. Murmuring echoed behind me.

"The angel-bond works on you?" the Duchess asked, surprised.

"Yes," I said through gritted teeth.

"What other angel-bond enchantments do you carry?" the Duke asked.

"Those are of a private nature, not for the masses' entertainment, and business contract related," I responded, attempting to make my tone of voice civil enough. "I have learned the hard way recently to be more careful who I make promises to."

"Who have you made promises to?" the Duchess asked.

"Mostly my mother and Viscount Kassian Oriel. The others are no longer valid."

"The Viscount put an oath on you?" the Duchess asked. "Kassian, what was this oath?"

"It is of a private nature; we do not need to question the young woman further. Truly, she has nothing to do with the current events plaguing angels," Kassian responded.

"Then why is she here? How did she get here?" the Duke asked.

"I brought her. I thought it would do her good. I see now it was a mistake," Kassian said quietly.

"Last I checked, we don't have a gift shop. We are not a museum, Kassian. We do not give tours to riff-raff off the street," Duke Manuel said.

"Well, maybe you should," I snapped at the Duke. Kassian glared at me with a harshness I had not seen since I first refused his hand in Tomas's office. It did nothing to cool my growing animosity toward the angels. "You sit up there on your high horses and judge me and judge him, but what have you done to help this city or the other cities in your control? All you truly care about are the angels. Only angels, and purebloods at that," I snarled. "The only riff-raff here is you—a bunch of distant regents with hearts of ice. The humans are not a lost cause, they never will be, but if you continue to treat them as such, I would not be surprised if they rise up to strike you down by any means necessary. I would."

CHAPTER 12

Silence was absolute for a moment, then chaos reigned. Angels jumped to their feet. Yelling ensued. Wings flared. No one made a move to strike at me, but I knew I had made a grave mistake when I saw Mercer and Kassian's faces. Mercer grinned at me, a wicked smile no one else noticed, but Kassian's expression was stoic. The warmth I had seen all night was gone, and in its place, a hardened warrior. I did not fear his reprisal so much as his displeasure; that much alone shocked me, but I would not budge.

I was right. To abandon the humans in the face of a conflict they were likely not involved with was wrong. Humans may have slighted me, bullied me, and made things harder than they needed to be, but half a city didn't deserve to be handed over to the demons on a silver platter.

Above the chaos of the chatter and the banging of a gavel, I heard a slow clap. It became louder and louder as the lords and ladies of the House settled down. At the end of the panel, an angel stood. Her purple wings were bright against her ivory dress, and she stepped down from her seat to join us on the House floor.

"Lords and ladies of the House, this *angel* speaks with the light and truth that her father did. While we did not always like what he had to say, he was right, as is his daughter. Humans need us more than ever, and we need them. Regents, work with your angels to protect them. Ensure that all legacies are well guarded against the darkness that is rising," the woman commanded. "Nora Evans, I'm glad to see you've found your voice. It has been a long time since you've been in these walls, child. I look forward to seeing you again, but I think it is best if you leave these halls now. Viscount Kassian, please remove your guest and meet me in my chambers when this meeting adjourns. We have much to discuss."

"Yes, Duchess, as you wish," Kassian said stiffly.

He approached me and grabbed my arm, not slowing his pace as he ushered me out of the hall. We didn't stop in the great hall where the Arcadian War looked down on us. He didn't stop his brutal stride until we were at the set of heavy wooden entrance doors we had avoided on our arrival. Two suited guards I didn't recognize from before opened the doors for us with barely a nod at Kassian.

The cool night air was brisk and harsh. The wind had picked up; another storm was on its way. Ahead of us were rows of limousines and town cars. A familiar-looking valet, Charlie, leaned against the hood of a black town car until he saw Kassian. Kassian stopped, only to yank open the door to the back seat. He flung his arm wide to gesture at the leather seats inside.

"Charlie, take Nora back to the Tower. Ensure she

gets to the penthouse safely. I'll find another way home. I'll be here awhile," Kassian said.

"Yes, sir. Miss Evans, please take a seat," Charlie said calmly.

"Kassian—" I started. He cut me a hard look.

"We'll discuss this later. Good night, Ms. Evans," Kassian said briskly. He turned and walked away without a second glance.

"It's best if you get in the car now, Nora. I don't know what happened in the House, but I can tell you a wicked storm is coming. I'd like to get off the road before it hits," Charlie said. I nodded mutely and ducked into the car. He shut the door behind me before going around and getting in on the driver's side.

"Are you comfortable?" Charlie asked, checking on me in the rearview mirror.

"Yes," I whispered.

"Do you mind if I put some music on?" he asked.

"No, go ahead," I responded.

Immediately, bluesy rock music played, then we pulled away from the curb, leaving the House and more than one angry angel behind.

Light from the mansion at our backs faded as we got farther and farther away and into the countryside. New Haven glowed in the distance like a dim light bulb beckoning us home. The movement lulled me to sleep more than once. Disoriented, I woke up when my head hit the window on the side of the car. We were surrounded by skyscrapers and streetlights. We were back in the city.

"Sorry, unavoidable pothole. I'll report it to the Transport Department. They'll have it fixed by the end of the week. Good news, we're almost back to the Tower," Charlie explained.

"It's okay," I mumbled and rubbed my head. Around me, the buildings looked familiar. "Have we been on this road before?"

"No, but the school is just ahead," Charlie said.

"School?"

"Your sister's school," Charlie said.

"Which side?" I asked as I unbuckled the seat belt and started looking out the windows.

"Up here on the left, the brownstone building," Charlie said as the car slowed down.

Most of the lights were off, but three floors up, a few windows were well lit from within. In one window was Lyra. She almost glowed in the night against all the darkness around her, and in her hands was a harp. I was glad to see she had come into possession of another harp, even though I couldn't hear a note, but I could tell she was playing. Her hands scrolled across the harp, back and forth, as she plucked the notes. Just knowing that she was in a place where she could play at any time of night brought some peace to my heart. Our neighbors hadn't always been the most understanding when it came to that. We rolled past the school slowly, and I suspected Charlie took this route on purpose for my benefit. It was a balm for my heart until I noticed I wasn't the only one watching Lyra. On the streets, two men stared up at her window and one of them had horns.

Demon.

"Charlie, there's a demon on the street staring at the school," I said.

The demon turned to look at our car as if he had

heard me. He likely did. Demons, like their angel counterparts, had heightened senses, twisted skills, and dark gifts.

"Not possible. This street is enchanted. Only angels and humans can be here," Charlie responded.

"I am telling you, there is a demon right there, without a doubt," I argued.

Charlie sighed and looked toward the school.

"There's nothing there, Nora. The night is playing tricks on you," Charlie said. There was no lie on his lips. He truly didn't see the men. The demon nodded his head at me as if he tipped his hat. Terror and rage gripped me. I wanted to fight them, confront them, and ensure my sister was truly safe.

"It's not a trick! You're the one being tricked!" I argued. I tried to push open the door, only to find it locked. I hit it in frustration, but it still didn't budge. I tried the window—nothing. "Let me out and I'll show you."

"No," Charlie said sternly.

He sped up, moving quickly away from the school even as I plastered my face to the back window. The demon and his partner turned their backs to us and walked away. The pair grew further and further away with each passing street lamp until they disappeared into the shadows completely.

I knew two facts at that moment. First, Lyra's school was not the haven the angels thought it was. Second, the angels sure as hell weren't to be trusted.

Charlie and I didn't speak the rest of the ride to the Tower. He parked in the garage, rode the elevator with me to the penthouse, and escorted me to the entrance. He wished me goodnight and was walking for the elevator before I could shut the door. I locked it and turned toward the guest room. Inside, a surprise waited. Stacks of my belongings lined the guest room wall, all organized and in brand new cardboard boxes. There were a few loose bags and a plant I suspected my sister insisted on sending. The ivy looked sad on the nightstand; there wasn't enough light in this room for it. I picked it up, turned around, and went in search of a better place for it. Someplace where the light would shine and give it everything it needed. The kitchen wasn't suited for the plant, because the kitchen island wouldn't get enough sun. The living room would be ideal, but there wasn't a ledge wide enough to support the hefty terracotta pot. There was only one other room left—Kassian's. I stared at that closed door for far longer than I should have.

"For the plant. I'm doing this for the plant," I whispered to the empty living room and my conscience. I grabbed the handle, half expecting it to be locked, but it opened easily beneath my fingers, revealing the massive four-poster bed inside. Everything about the room was big, from the bed to the swords mounted on the wall, and the balcony which opened to the night sky, being perfect for the plant. "For the plant," I repeated.

I slowly walked to the balcony. My eyes scanned the room to see what I could learn of the Viscount.

Unlike the rest of the apartment, the furniture in this room looked old. The wood was polished from use, not vanity. Open doors to an office, large closet, and bathroom hinted at similar design choices to the rest of the penthouse suite and a wardrobe of all black. Simple, warm, and understated, except for the additional swords and rows of leather-bound books that peeked out from the office doorway. I slid open the glass door to the balcony while balancing the pot on my hip. Leaving the door open, I stepped out into a lush getaway. Lyra's plant would have company, at least. I found the perfect empty spot on a side table for it. With the plant safe and secure with its own brethren, I felt even more like I was trespassing, but the space was also a comfort.

High above the city, Kassian had his own little oasis tucked away. It reminded me of our reading nook at home with all of Lyra's plants. The garden rooftop seemed less of an oddity now as I slipped my hands over the cool metal banister railing. The plants danced in the growing evening wind. Even though I couldn't see it, I could tell the storm was almost here. The air had that charged, heavy feeling before the skies opened up and the fury of a storm unleashed itself on the city. A warm body pressed up against me, pinning me to the banister as a pair of masculine hands covered mine. The urge to fight rose within me. I felt angel-light rushing to the surface, ready to hurt the man who dared put their hands on me.

"What are you doing in my room, little angel?" Kassian whispered into my ear. The building fury in my blood melted away. "Don't you think you've caused enough trouble tonight?"

"Kassian," I breathed, as I fought to compose my warring emotions. Adrenaline still coursed through my blood. My heart raced as I tried to get my breathing under control. "I didn't hear you."

"I didn't want you to," he whispered. "Why are you here? I may not have your gift of truth, but believe me, I can tell if you're lying."

"My sister," I said, and his hands tightened across mine.

"What about her?" he asked.

"She sent me one of our plants. It needed a safe place with light. It would have died in my room without her touch," I explained as his hands relaxed, his thumbs softly stroking mine.

"The recent addition on the left," Kassian stated.

"Yes," I responded.

"I'll keep it safe, little angel, but I'm still furious with you," Kassian admitted, his voice heavy with emotion even as he moved away from me, allowing me to put some distance between my body and the banister.

"Was the House of Lords angry?" I asked as he stepped away completely back toward his bedroom. I immediately noticed the lack of his body heat. The night air was brisk, with the temperature dropping.

"Livid. They wanted a full inquiry into you and your sister," Kassian responded.

"My sister has nothing to do—"

"Which is exactly what I told them. Your sister is safe, even if you seem determined to get yourself tossed into the Pit," Kassian said and released my captive hands. He ran his hands through his windswept, and rain-soaked hair in frustration. He had flown home, his wings sagged, the tips touching the floor behind him.

"Thank you," I responded. He groaned.

"I shouldn't have taken you. I spent the last hour flying, trying to clear my head. I don't know whether to be furious that you put the House in its place, or to kiss you because you're right and absolutely radiant. Either way, you shouldn't have had to be the one to stand up for the humans. The House of Commons should have been there to speak for themselves," Kassian said.

"Why weren't they called?" I asked.

"The Duchess didn't say, only that the tides are shifting. Many angels want to overrule humans, not move forward into equality. The House likely decided it wasn't a human issue and left them out of it. Or they truly believe humans are at fault and felt they were a security threat," Kassian rambled on.

"Humans respect power. Give them power, control, and an objective, and you would be surprised what they can accomplish on their own. If the angels don't step up and give humans what they want, the demons will, and then you will have a problem on your hands," I suggested and shrugged my shoulders. Kassian chuckled in response and nodded his head in agreement.

"What?" I asked as I leaned against the banister. Kassian stepped closer. He used the edge of his hand to tilt my head up. He looked at me as if he could see into my soul. I hoped he couldn't see the truth burning there.

"I should have let you tear those ancients apart. You, Nora Evans, see things as they are, not as people want them to be," Kassian whispered. His head ducked closer, his lips crashing into mine, hot and demanding.

The kiss snapped the control I had over the emotions warring within. I kissed him back as his hands dropped to mine on the banister, keeping me pinned there as he dominated my mouth. His body pressed against mine. Everywhere we touched, heat and desire bloomed. The kiss was everything that had been brewing between us all night made physical—every taunt, hint, and tease. Everything I had refused to admit from the moment I started dressing to impress him. He was the angel I wanted to fall from grace. I'll be damned, but I wanted to fall with him.

A battle of passion warred between us as lightning cracked the sky, and it began to rain. Cold water hit us from above, the wind teasing and pulling at my clothes and hair. I desperately wanted to touch him, but his hands kept mine firmly in place until they were suddenly free. His hands dropped to my waist and pulled me close against his body, away from the banister and into his room, out of the falling rain. He groaned as his hands slipped lower and gripped my hips in a tight squeeze. He broke the kiss first. His head rested on my shoulder for a moment as he froze.

"Tell me you don't want this, little angel, and it ends right here, right now. On my wings, I swear this is your choice," Kassian said with reverence and I felt the tendrils of an angel oath connect us. For an angel to swear on their wings was one of the strongest promises they could make, only superseded by an oath on their soul.

"Don't you dare stop now," I responded, and his promise wrapped around me and melded with the oldest deal in my being. A promise I had foolishly made before I knew what they meant, before I understood what being an angel meant, or that I'd ever have wings of my own.

"You can say no and walk away. I will not hold it against you," Kassian said.

"Shut up and ravish me, archangel," I ordered with a smile.

CHAPTER 13

"Thank Arcadia," Kassian whispered in relief before he kissed along my neck as he worked my dress up over my hips. I reached my hands out around him and trailed them along the tops of his wings. Kassian trembled at my touch and groaned in pleasure. He used his teeth to nip at my throat before returning to kissing me.

"Take care of how you play with my wings, little angel. A man can only take so much torture."

Kassian's hands slipped beneath the hem of my dress, caressing my skin as he slowly worked the silky fabric up and over my body. Not to be rushed, he continued to trail kisses up and down the sensitive flesh along my neck and exposed shoulder until he had to pull the fabric over my head. He stopped and moved out of my arms to look at me. I felt the loss of his touch keenly, suddenly aware I stood in only my thigh-high boots, the gold bangle on my wrist, and scraps of black lace snug against my most intimate parts.

"You're a magnificent creature," Kassian whispered. His hazel eyes seemed to glow from within for a second, as if the fire of his desire was surging along with his power. The timbre of his voice struck a chord in my core, making it clench in response. Kassian represented everything I despised and craved. I would fall for him. I had fallen for him. That old angel oath hummed within. It recognized what I wasn't ready to admit.

I winked at Kassian and leaned low to unzip one boot, then the other, stepping out of them. A fake groan of unhappiness escaped the man across from me.

"I liked the boots; maybe next time," Kassian suggested with a grin.

"You assume there will be a next time?" I responded coyly with a grin of my own. He laughed in turn and reached for me.

"Come here, you minx. I'll ensure there's a next time," he promised.

Kassian scooped me up in his arms and tossed me onto the middle of his bed. The mattress was firm but cushioned my landing. He began stripping out of his clothes and vanishing his wings. I pouted.

"I liked the wings," I admitted sheepishly.

"Next time," Kassian said. My response died on my lips as he continued to strip, revealing inch after inch of sun-kissed skin and muscles until all that was left was the black denim jeans hanging off his hips. "Are you sure, little angel?"

I hesitated a moment, focusing on where his hips tapered to a chiseled V. Kassian froze, waiting for a response. His eyes glowed in the dim light, a smug smirk played at his lips.

"Don't keep me waiting, archangel. I've waited long enough," I said as my body tensed with anticipation, but he didn't hesitate.

He stalked up onto the bed, kneeling between my legs. He gently used his hands to push me down onto the mattress before palming my breasts. I arched into the touch, desperate for more through the sheer lace cups. He shoved my bra down, exposing my nipples to the cool air and his touch. They pebbled in response. I gasped as he captured one in his mouth while twisting the other between his fingers. He used his free hand to grip my hips and tug me up against his. There was no mistaking the throbbing heat pressed against the lace of my panties.

He ground against me softly, causing a quiet moan to leave my lips. Kassian laughed against my breast before pulling back and resting on his knees, his fingers trailing down my stomach and brushing along the skin to the hem of my panties.

"You approve," Kassian whispered huskily as one hand continued down my thigh. His other hand moved the thin fabric to the side. The heat in his eyes was unmistakable as he looked me over. I felt as if I could stare at him forever. Except my eyes fluttered shut as his thumb brushed along my clit with ease, causing me to buck my hips in response.

He rubbed gentle circles that had me writhing and biting on my lip, needing more than what he was giving. My body warmed as I grew closer and closer to an inevitable orgasm.

Leaning forward, his warm lips met my skin just below my belly button as both hands found my panties and pulled them down. As they reached my knees, he lifted off of me again, taking my panties off, and as I opened my eyes, I caught him tossing them to the side. His thumb once again found my center as his brilliant eyes bore straight into mine before they once again fell shut, my body responding to him of its own accord.

"More, I want more," I demanded and dragged my fingers along the bed, needing something to grip on to. When I found nothing but the soft sheets below me, I reached forward to grab him instead. Tugging him forward, his warm, firm chest landed on mine, the heat of his body both overwhelming and welcome.

"I'll give you everything you want and more, little angel," Kassian murmured. His hand came up to brush some hair away from my face right before he leaned down to press his lips against mine in a soft, sweet kiss. Shifting his hips, I felt his hardness slide along me. I shivered in response just as the soft tip found my entrance, and his hips urged forward—only to freeze.

"Don't stop now," I gritted.

"You're a—" Kassian started.

"Kassian, I will never forgive you if you stop now," I hissed. He pursed his lips, pulled back, and thrust forward again, this time not stopping against the resistance as my body adjusted to accommodate his size. Pleasure and pain twinned at once within me, sending me over the edge as he reached between us to tease my clit and capture my lips with his. I felt the tendrils of the old angel oath burn brightly as he ravished me through my orgasm. My angel-light unleashed and flashed brilliantly in the room like an overcharged bulb. He paused for a moment, his eyes shining as he stared down at me. A smirk overtook the surprise on his face after unraveling another of my mysteries, while my body hummed and trembled with wave after wave of pleasure.

"Keeping secrets, little angel?" Kassian whispered as he gently kept thrusting. The smirk fell from his lips. "Are you sure?"

"Ravish me, archangel, ravish me," I whispered as I pulled him down on top of me.

Kassian took me, again and again, until we were both spent. Even then, he picked me up gently and carried me into his adjoining bathroom.

"Your pick, shower or bath?" he asked.

"Shower," I responded. He set me on the edge of the tub and turned the faucets to start the water.

"The toilet is through that door if you need it. Take your time. I'll be right back to join you in the shower," Kassian said, turning to leave me in the bathroom alone. He turned back and kissed me gently on the lips. "We will talk about what happened back there, but regardless—thank you for trusting me, Nora."

Then the archangel was gone. After quickly taking care of my basic needs, I stepped into the shower and washed the traces of our lovemaking away. Kassian returned and joined me in the shower; his warm, callused hands trailed across the tops of my shoulders before skimming along my body and returning to my shoulders to work at the knots.

"Why didn't you tell me you were inexperienced? That's really something you should tell a man," Kassian said softly. "I would have done things differently."

"I enjoyed it and wouldn't have changed it. Plus, I figured you heard the rumors and knew. Tomas clearly laid it out at the auction, and I'm not wholly inexperienced," I responded. That failed night with Micheal years ago flashed through my mind. The memory was still bittersweet.

"People lie. I figured it was part of his sales pitch. Why'd you wait?" Kassian asked. "You must have had suitors at some point."

"It wasn't for lack of trying. I accidentally made an angel oath with my mother one day. It's prevented me from getting experience with just anyone," I responded. Kassian froze.

"Your mother made you give an angel bond to maintain your chastity?" Kassian said, his tone suggested disbelief and a touch of horror. I laughed.

"No, I made one by accident when I fancied I'd end up in a love story like my parents. Last I checked, there wasn't a way to release an angel or demon from an oath. At least, not that my mother could find," I said.

"Sometimes, there are loopholes. What was the oath?" Kassian asked.

"I'm not telling you," I responded.

"Come on, please?" Kassian begged playfully.

"No," I said sternly.

"Okay," Kassian said. "When were you going to tell me you had angel-light?"

"When the time was right," I responded evasively.

"Any other gifts I should be aware of? Or surprises to look out for?"

"I'll let you know," I teased. He nipped at my earlobe playfully.

"Don't keep me in the dark too long, little angel," Kassian warned before he kissed my neck. By the end, we needed another shower. Kassian was quick to give me one of his shirts to wear, as if I were too much of a temptation in only a towel. He had no such reservations about himself with a black towel draped low across his waist. He took me in his arms and kissed me again.

"We should get some sleep. Stay with me tonight?" Kassian asked.

"Of course," I responded. This time, his kiss was soft, gentle, and full of tenderness. It was a slow, sweet surrender I had never expected from an archangel until it wasn't and he was slowly maneuvering us back to the bed. He guided me backward until my legs hit the edges of the mattress. His hands drifted to the bottom of his t-shirt at my thighs when the door to his bedroom opened.

"Kass—" the intruder started, only to be interrupted by Kassian's growl. Kassian's wings appeared, spread wide to shield me from sight as he turned toward the intruder. I looked over a dark burgundy wing to find an angel standing there, amused, as Kassian adjusted the towel at his waist. The angel looked from Kassian to me and back before grinning even more at the development.

"Well, don't you two look cozy," Silas drawled. "Guess that rose has been plucked after all."

CHAPTER 14

"You better have a damn good reason for barging into my bedroom using your shadow gift, Silas, or I swear I will eventually find a rune that will lock you out," Kassian growled. The smile on Silas's face faltered and grim seriousness took over. I scanned the room for my scattered clothing as Kassian approached Silas.

"You weren't picking up your phone. Now I can see why, but it couldn't wait, Kass. We found Helena. Icarus is keeping her stable, but she'll pass out soon," Silas said. Kassian cursed.

"Where is she now?" Kassian asked.

"She's downstairs, waiting for you with the others. They broke her," Silas said. Kassian cursed again.

"Turn around, Silas." Kassian ordered. Silas did so without hesitation. Kassian handed me the towel from his waist to cover myself with, then went to his closet to pull out fresh clothes and dressed quickly.

"Nora, get dressed. You're coming with us," Kassian ordered, all the softness in his demeanor gone. In its place, the Viscount of New Haven and warrior of Arcadia reigned. I wrapped the towel tightly around my body and skirted past Silas. He gave me a terse nod, giving nothing away. I ran to my room and grabbed the first outfit within reach before returning to the men where they met me in the hallway. It was a brisk walk to the elevator. The doors opened, and we stepped inside. I was incredibly aware of how small I was compared to the two angels with their wings out, competing for space. Torn between bumping into Kassian and maintaining a sense of distance, I gave in and stepped closer to him.

"What do you know?" Kassian asked as Silas pushed a button, prompting the elevator to begin its descent.

"Not much. Humans found her in a ditch in the warehouse district in East Haven," Silas said. "Not far from Bookie Tomas's grounds."

"Whoever dumped her knew we cleared out that section. It would be unwatched," Kassian responded bitterly as Silas nodded in agreement.

"She's barely alive, Kass," Silas said.

"Has she said anything?"

"She's asking for you, mercy, and forgiveness," Silas said tersely. The elevator slowed, the door opening on a floor I hadn't been to. In front of us was an empty secretary's desk. To the left and right were hallways leading to a collection of doors.

"It's bad, Kassian. The damage... Are you sure Nora can handle it?" Silas asked, looking at me sadly. "There are some things young angels shouldn't see." Kassian gave me an assessing look as he appeared to weigh the options of leaving me behind.

"Where are we?" I asked. "Why am I here?"

"The infirmary," Kassian responded. "I need to know the truth in case she's been turned against us or cursed. If you can't handle it, you can leave."

"I'll come," I said, resolved not to flinch at whatever atrocity I was about to witness.

"Follow me," Silas said.

He led us down the hall to a harshly lit room. Inside stood Mercer, still in his business attire. Beside him stood Celeste, though she was dressed casually in loungewear, her hair up in a messy bun, and a sewer's pin cushion still strapped to her wrist. Celeste did not seem surprised to see me, but Mercer certainly did. He scowled at me while Icarus was hunched over a broken female angel lying on a cot. She was lying face down; her sea-foam green wings were scorched and bleeding. Icarus was packing the burns with medication and bandages. The smell of burned feathers and flesh made my stomach flip, and I fought the urge to run from the room to avoid it. A once beautiful but broken and bruised angel looked up from the bed, the dirt on her face streaked with tears, but her golden eyes shone brightly as she focused on Kassian and tried to raise her body from the bed. Icarus's firm hand at the top of her shoulders kept her on the bed.

"Don't move, Helena. I'm not done," Icarus said gently.

"Kassian, forgive me. I'm sorry, I'm so sorry," Helena pleaded as she sagged back onto the bed even as she held a bandaged hand out to Kassian.

"Her hand is healed. You can take it," Icarus said softly when Kassian hesitated. He stepped forward and took her outstretched hand. Icarus stepped away to make room, taking his supplies with him.

"She's stable for now. Take care," Icarus said. "Don't move more than you need to, Helena."

"Helena, how did you make it back to us?" Kassian asked. "Who took you? How?"

"I was making my rounds. I didn't see their faces. They wore masks but smelled human and demon," Helena said. "They thought I was dead when they dropped my body. They are based in East Haven, and where they dropped me wasn't far from the warehouse, they kept me in."

"Was it for sport or information?" Mercer asked. "What did they want? What did you give them?"

The broken angel sobbed.

"Helena, what can you tell me?" Kassian asked quietly.

"Forgive me, Kass, forgive me," Helena pleaded again.

"Always, Helena. What did they want?" Kassian asked as Mercer paced in his corner.

"They wanted to know about you and the Tower. How to get in, get out, and weaknesses," Helena explained, and Kassian's shoulders relaxed. He didn't seem concerned about an assault on the Tower, which made me wonder if he was more worried about a door to hell being opened with the information Helena knew.

"If they intend to come for me, I'll make sure to dress the part," Kassian said jokingly, trying to lighten the mood, but Helena only cried harder.

"It's not just you and this tower. They're going after the House of Lords, all our security strongholds, and the children," Helena sobbed. She twisted and pushed herself up off the bed to look at Kassian, her eyes wide with fear. "They're going after all the families and children!" Helena screamed as she clutched at Kassian's shirt. Her eyes rolled into the back of her head, her hands going slack as she fell unconscious. Kassian caught her and set her back on the bed. Icarus stepped up beside him, a syringe in his hands.

"A sedative to keep her asleep while she heals," Icarus said, waiting for Kassian's approval. Kassian nodded stiffly.

"Everyone meet me in the hall," Kassian said, and I turned to exit the room. "Nora, Icarus, both of you stay." Silas and Celeste exited without hesitation. They both seemed relieved to leave the room. Mercer, though, glared at me with narrowed eyes before slowly taking his time to move into the hall. Celeste smirked at Mercer and pointedly shut the door behind him. I turned back to Kassian. His face was hard. His lips pressed into the thinnest line. He looked older.

"Is Helena telling the truth?" Kassian asked darkly, his eyes brimming with fury. There was no hint of a lie in the room, no suggestion that anything was false about what the broken angel had claimed.

"Helena is telling the truth as far as she knows," I responded. "You should know, I saw something on the way to the Tower from the House of Lords. Charlie took me to my sister's school. There were demons on the street looking up at her."

"Did you tell Charlie?" Kassian asked.

"He said the school was warded, that it was impossible for them to be there, but I know what I saw," I affirmed.

"Charlie is right. Celeste wards all three of the boarding schools herself. Your sister is safe," Icarus responded, and Kassian nodded in acknowledgement.

"Icarus is right. Your sister is safe. You healed your

mother and sister all those years ago. Do you think you can heal her with your light?" Kassian asked as he waved a hand in Helena's direction. Icarus's startled intake of breath in the room was audible over the broken angel's labored breathing.

"You have your father's gift," Icarus whispered in awe.

"I can help heal the worst injury, but I've never been able to do what I did for my mother again. I—" I stumbled over my words as they became stuck in my throat. "I couldn't stop the cancer."

Icarus reached a hand out and touched my shoulder gently.

"Angel-light has its limits, Nora. We all wish it didn't, but it does. If you could mend her wings at all, it will make her healing less traumatic and mean the world to Helena," Icarus said.

I held my hand over the worst looking spot on her wings. The broken bones Icarus had been attempting to set properly seemed the best spot to work. I closed my eyes and focused on the light within, on the hope, on my wish to fly. If I could heal the bones, her seafoam wings might become strong enough to be weight bearing. Through my closed eyes, I still saw my hands glow and grow hot as the light spread. I let it flow until I became lightheaded. I swayed and Kassian's hands caught me around the shoulders and pulled me back from the broken angel. I opened my eyes. His face hovered over mine. His concerned eyes flickered back and forth over me. I closed my eyes tight as a wave of vertigo overwhelmed me.

"Did it work? Was it enough?" I asked.

"Yes, little angel, thank you," Kassian said, kindness and adoration carried in the tone of his voice.

"More than enough. Look, Nora," Icarus whispered in excitement and relief. I looked at Helena. She breathed deeply, peacefully. The spot I had attempted to heal was whole, and not only that spot but both her wings gleamed fully healed, with not a single burned feather.

"Icarus, Celeste can know but no one else" Kassian ordered.

"Of course. I'll watch over Helena myself. Thank you, Nora. Your parents would be so proud," Icarus said as he patted my arm, but returned his entire focus to the patient in his care. He pulled a curtain around Helena to block her from prying eyes. A hand banged on the door. Kassian opened it, a dark gaze on Mercer.

"Mercer, Celeste—call a war room meeting. Notify all the archangels you can. There's been a security breach. Lock the tower down. Angels can only come and go through the roof," Kassian ordered. "Nora, you're coming with us."

"Do you think it is wise bringing that halfling into the war room?" Mercer asked. Kassian paused and looked back at me. I was surprised by the shadow of doubt that crossed his face for a moment before it hardened.

"We need her. She needs us. She's in as much danger now as the rest of us," Kassian said.

The war room was less intimidating than it sounded. Along the walls were rows of chairs, but in the center of the room was a model of the city. Various areas of the city were color-coded. I recognized East End immediately, the entire area lit with green. To the south, red engulfed the city with scattered clusters of green. The north side of New Haven was a mix of yellow and green. Arcadian Tower, along with a few other buildings, was blue. At the edge of the model city, throughout the countryside, was a scattering of blue and yellow lights. The House of Lords and House of Commons were easy to pinpoint. The model table was surrounded by stools. Kassian stood at the head of the table and beckoned me over.

"This is a model of New Haven. The green represents known human populations, red light represents demons, yellow light represents angels, and blue identifies the most valuable angel strongholds. There are well over two dozen across New Haven," Kassian explained.

"What makes them valuable?" I asked as the other angels took their seats around the table.

"Money, weapons, archangel homes, strongholds, and our children," Kassian responded. He pointed his finger to a solitary blue light along a street between Arcadian Tower and East End. "That's your sister's boarding school, for example. There are multiple high value buildings throughout the north side of the city." Kassian moved closer to me, leaning close to whisper in my ear. "Take a seat along the wall and listen to what everyone has to say. I need you to pay attention to what we talked about before. Only an insider could have orchestrated Helena's abduction." Kassian stepped away from me and took a seat.

I did as he instructed and watched as angels entered through the elevator. Their looks, clothing, and wing coloration varied; if they had mates, they weren't present. All the angels had the same determined demeanor. These were all powerful angels. I suspected they were all archangels. There were no amiable smiles among the group. Curt nods and stiff handshakes were as cordial as they got when greeting the other angels gathered. Some were taken aback when they saw me sitting along the wall; others merely nodded at me. A few looked familiar, and I realized I had seen them at The Feather only hours before. Soon, the table was nearly full and only a handful of seats remained empty. Kassian stood.

"Brothers and sisters, New Haven is in danger. From what and who, exactly, we do not know," Kassian started. Grumbling echoed around the table. Kassian raised his hand, and the table fell silent. "The House has been notified. I've brought you here today, not for war, but so we can protect New Haven as a whole."

"Why do you think New Haven is in danger? What have you heard, Viscount?" one angel asked. The angel was dressed casually in blue jeans and a green dress shirt, his hair a mess as though he just tumbled from bed.

"Helena has been recovered. She was found in the East End. She was tortured for information regarding the tower, our strongholds, and families," Kassian responded. An outcry erupted across the table. Magic flared so strongly, halos and auras shone around some of the angels as their emotions raged.

"Why did you call us all here?" another angel hissed. Like others around the table, his appearance was a bit ill-kept, as if he had dressed in haste. His long red hair was pulled back into a taunt, unbrushed knot and his shirt was wrinkled. "You've left our mates, our families defenseless!"

"We don't know when they will strike. I wanted to tell you all at once, in person, so there was no confusion. We need to move quickly to secure the families and assets. Everyone with children should move their families into the strongholds in their sectors. Until we have a good idea of what they want, we are stronger together." Kassian responded.

"Who are they?" the angel in the green asked.

"Could be demons, could be humans—it's most likely both," Silas answered.

"You would know, wouldn't you, demon halfling?" the red-haired angel snarled. "Shouldn't you be in the Pit keeping that scum in check?"

Silas's eyes darkened to inky black, but he did not retaliate. He simply tilted his head and stared at the angel.

"When the Viscount calls me, I come," Silas said coolly.

"Like a good little pet," the hot-headed angel hissed.

"Koriel, enough!" Kassian ordered, his jaw clenched in frustration, and flames erupted around his closed hands.

"What would you have us do, Kass?" a soft-spoken female angel asked. Around her head, a halo burned, matching the fire in her eyes.

"Those of you with families, take them and protect them. Go now, leave the city. Notify the lower angels in your networks, especially if they have families. The House should already be making arrangements in other cities for you. When we have more information, Celeste or I will contact you. Trust no one. May you fly fast and true," Kassian ordered. Half the table rose without a word and left the room without hesitation. Only twelve angels remained, their faces stoic.

"That was reckless, Viscount. There aren't enough archangels without families to protect the city on our own," Mercer said. Celeste's phone rang. Half the table looked over at Celeste as she stepped away to answer it. She looked worried. "There are twelve of us and three dozen sites at risk."

"Half of those are enchanted and protected from demons. We focus on the ones that aren't," Kassian said.

"What if it's not the demons we should be worried about?" Mercer enquired.

"Then we'll deal with the humans," Kassian responded.

"Which sites do you want to focus on?" Silas questioned.

"We should focus on Arcadian weapons and our strongholds. If we lose those to the demons, they'll have a foothold in the city until we can get reinforcements. Two of us need to stay at the Tower. The rest of us will divide up the city and protect what we can," Kassian said.

"What about the schools?" I asked.

"Celeste wards them herself," Mercer said in an annoyed tone. "Let the real angels talk." I rolled my eyes at the pompous angel.

"If the demons can get into the Tower, then they probably have a plan to get into the schools. I saw one outside my sister's school hours ago. What are you doing to protect the students?" I asked.

"The schools are warded. We'll engage safety measures for the schools the same as we did for the families. Don't worry, Nora, the teachers will protect their students, including your sister." Kassian said nothing but the truth.

"Silas, return to the Pit. Take Meloiah with you. Make sure the demons in the Pit don't take this opportunity to stage an escape," Kassian ordered. Silas and a brute of a warrior angel rose from the table. Meloiah had materialized a battle ax that he now slung over his shoulder, his wings a bright orange.

"Chaliel and Brual, pull the guard and watch over these buildings in the north side," Kassian said, pointing to a cluster of blue lights on the north side of town. "Do not let them fall into demons' hands."

Celeste stepped back to the table, her face grave.

"That was Eretria. Half of the lower East End is burning. Humans and demons are targeting the outreach programs and the warehouse district. Calls are coming in from the south side of North Haven. Lower angels are being threatened by humans," Celeste said, a harsh truth.

"Koriel, go to the south side and help the angels there," Kassian ordered.

"And the enemy?" Koriel questioned.

"What about the enemy?" Kassian responded.

"Detain or kill?" Koriel asked briskly, a warrior preparing for his assignment.

"Use your best judgment. Save as many angels as you can, spare the humans if possible. They may be demon possessed," Kassian answered. "Mercer, warn your people in the financial district. If humans are rising against angels, they'll likely make their way there. Then go to the House of Lords. Give them whatever assistance they require."

"Don't you think I should stay in the city, by your side?" Mercer asked.

"No, protect your people. Then go to the House. I

need someone there that can tell me how they want to respond," Kassian explained.

"As you wish, Viscount," Mercer said before rising from the table. "I trust your judgment." The first hint of a lie.

"Gavinel and Pilos, go to the warehouse district. See what can be salvaged. Save who you can," Kassian said. Both men rose and left without a word.

"Celeste, Icarus—I need you to stay here at the Tower with Eretria. Tell me what is going on," Kassian said. "Rodelia and I will deal with the fires in the East End."

"The fires are likely just a distraction," Icarus said. "The warehouse district is not as valuable as the strongholds. They're trying to pull us away from what matters, Kass. Don't make the same mistake I did." Icarus spoke the truth, as much as it hurt to hear. The warehouse district meant nothing to the angels. Still, it was the lifeblood of the East End and flanked entire neighborhoods—my neighborhood. Kassian looked at me, his face stern.

"We cannot abandon the humans to burn," Kassian responded. "We are meant to protect the humans, to coexist with them. If we do not save the East End, the humans will forever rise against us, and everything New Haven was meant to be will be lost in the aftermath."

"What about the rest of the strongholds?" Celeste asked.

"The enchantments will hold. They have to," Kassian responded. "There is no other option."

CHAPTER 15

Celeste left the war room to join Eretria on silent steps with no further discussion. Rodelia followed her to get a list of the targeted outreach programs, while Kassian stood alone at the table, staring at the model of the city. He leaned forward on fisted palms as he stared at the city. His eyes flickered back and forth between the areas of interest to him. Instead of relief, he appeared even tenser than before. His jaw was clenched, his eyebrows furrowed.

"Did any of them lie?" Kassian asked quietly.

"No," I answered. "They were all truthful with their words, though I'm not sure I trusted most of them. What are you looking at?"

"Where to put you, where to keep you safe," Kassian responded.

"I'm not going with you to the East End?" I asked, surprised.

"Unless you're hiding angel-fire or healing-water from me, I'm not taking you into an inferno and an angry mob of humans bent on attacking angels," Kassian responded. A part of me cringed. I had a form of angelfire, but I could never control it. It was unreliable and unwieldy. I had almost burned our home to the ground. I'd likely make the fire worse if I went with him.

"You want me to stay here?" I questioned, but Kassian shook his head no.

"I'm sending you to a different stronghold. You'll be safer there. The Tower isn't warded against demons," Kassian explained. "Your sister's school is, and you should be with your family tonight. I'll take you myself."

"Thank you," I said. I took his head in my hands and kissed him chastely. A simple kiss goodbye, yet a promise for all the conversations we needed to have at some point, but needed to wait. "The city burns; we should go."

"The others can handle a few minutes without me. I'm not sending you out into a burning city defenseless. I'm taking you to get geared up first, then we'll go together," Kassian responded. He grabbed my hand and led me to the elevator.

"How's that feel?" Kassian asked as he cinched another strap tightly against my body. The leather Kassian fitted over my clothes was thick, heavy, and cumbersome.

"Like you've strapped a sack of potatoes and a wooden board to my back," I responded and twisted my body, trying to get some mobility back. Kassian grumbled as he undid the straps and stomped back into the closet. He came out with a pile of metal chains in his hands.

"This will have to work," Kassian said. "I'm not giving you a weapon; without proper training, it would likely be used against you. You shouldn't need anything, anyway. The school is protected and the teachers are warriors themselves."

"Then why are we in the armory?" I questioned, the image of demons standing on the sidewalk outside my sister's school still top of mind. The sooner I was with Lyra, the better.

"To give me peace of mind, and uphold my side of the deal to take care of you, little angel," Kassian said pointedly as he lifted the chain toward me.

"What is it?" I asked as Kassian hefted the metal over my head, still wishing he would at least consider giving me a knife. It weighed as much as the leather, but allowed me slightly more movement. He pulled a leather belt off his shoulder and strapped it around my waist. The metal formed an unflattering metal tunic down to my knees. Clearly, it was never intended for a person my size.

"My armor. It's the best there is, and it'll have to do. It should protect you against demon enchantment and most powers. There's nothing else left," Kassian explained before he fit his own weapons to his body around his wings. "I need to stop by the penthouse and retrieve my swords. I'll drop you outside the school, and I'll check on you later."

"If I'm wearing your armor, what are you wearing?" I asked as we strode to the elevator.

"This," Kassian gestured to himself. "I don't need

enchantments against fire. Fire is my element. It bends to me, I do not bow before it."

"And the demons?" I asked as the door slid open. He grinned.

"I'll burn them before they get close. This isn't the first time New Haven has burned, but hopefully, it'll be the last," Kassian said. "Follow me, stay close."

The elevator doors opened onto the penthouse floor. Kassian ran down the hallway, not looking back to ensure I followed behind him. Together we ran through the penthouse, back into the room where the smell of our lovemaking still floated in the air. He grabbed the blades off the wall and walked to the balcony before securing them to the harness wrapped around his wings. He paused and looked back at me. His eyes glowed at the edges like embers.

"Fly with me?" Kassian asked as he reached out a hand to me. I took it, and he pulled me up into his arms, launching us into the sky without hesitation. He cussed, and I looked around us. The city glowed, but not with early dawn light.

The city burned. Almost all of East End was on fire.

Kassian's wings beat against the smokey air as he carried us swiftly to the steps of the Lyra's school. He set me on the ground roughly; our landing was hasty.

"Go inside, find your sister. Stay safe. Trust no one," Kassian ordered. He ducked his head swiftly and stole a kiss. Without waiting for a response, he stepped back and launched himself into the air, flying toward the raging inferno. Even from the ground, you could see the growing angry glow of the fire as it ate through the city.

I turned to the brownstone building beside me. Every window glowed with light in the early morning darkness. The school no longer slept and was on guard. I could see more than one person pacing back and forth in front of their window. I approached the school and knocked on the old wooden door before I noticed the doorbell. I pushed the button; a chime echoed behind the door. A muffled response sounded before a small opening appeared in the door, and the eyes of an old woman peered out.

"What's your name? What business do you have here?" she asked fiercely.

"Nora Evans, sister of Lyra Evans. Viscount Kassian sent me," I answered. The window in the door slid shut, and I heard a series of locks being undone before the door swung open enough to let me in. I stepped inside quickly. The woman closed the door behind me, the locks clicking back in place with a wave of her hand. The angel wings on her back were small, and pitch-black, streaked with gray.

"Icarus said you would be on your way. Welcome, daughter of Ramiel. My name is Rachiel," the old woman said. "The school is on alert in case the fire spreads in this direction. Many of our pupils are being fetched by their families to the countryside until the city cools off and the archangels have dealt with the situation. Your sister is waiting for you at the top of the stairs. She has a beautiful gift of music."

I looked up at the grand staircase, and at the top of the stairs, I saw a mop of hair and green eyes I recognized looking over the edge of the staircase banister. Bright emerald eyes that matched my own watched my every step as I climbed the stairs. Lyra descended the staircase to meet me.

"Nora!" Lyra cried, and her arms wrapped around me and clutched me tight over the heavy chain mail.

"Lyra," I whispered into her hair as I hugged her back. She wore a school uniform I didn't recognize, with a satchel across her shoulders. She smelled of laundry softener and her plants. I hugged her tighter as the old angel approached us.

"It has been a pleasure getting to know Lyra. I'd like to get to know you as well, Miss Nora. I fear it'll be a long night. Most of the teachers are busy with their assigned wards. Would you two like to join me for hot chocolate in the parlor?" Rachiel asked as she gestured to a room off the staircase.

"What do you say, Lyra?" I asked softly, just grateful that my sister was okay. Lyra smiled brightly with delight at the prospect of hot chocolate.

"They make fantastic hot chocolate; they add cinnamon just like mom did," Lyra said.

"Your father liked it that way, too," Rachiel said with a wink.

"We would be thankful for a cup or two, Miss Rachiel." I accepted her offer with a smile. The old woman nodded and smiled in turn. She seemed sincere, which was reassuring in its own way. I needed to work on my own prejudices against angels. At this rate, maybe it was only archangels that were snobs.

"Come along, ladies." Rachiel began a slow descent back down the stairs, and we followed her into the parlor. "I'll be right back. Please make yourself comfortable. You can take that dreaded metal off, if you'd like. The school is protected, and we're in lockdown. Only an archangel or myself can open the doors, unless a child is at risk."

"That's good to hear," I acknowledged as I sat on a velvet evergreen settee that seemed ancient but comfortable. Lyra plopped down beside me.

"Do you know Icarus?" Lyra inquired suddenly with rapt curiosity.

"Yes, why?" I asked as Lyra pulled her satchel onto her lap. It was new, like her uniform. She opened the bag and pulled out a golden harp. The harp from our mother, rebuilt. She held it out to me, and without pause, I took it from her gently. It had been painstakingly pieced together. What wasn't perfectly mended appeared to be held together with gold.

"Icarus came to see me after he fixed it. He said it would never be the same, but it would be stronger and play true for me," Lyra said. "He said our lives would never be the same, but we would be stronger for it, too. Do you think he was telling the truth?"

"Have you played it?" I asked with a soft smile. Lyra shook her head, her eyes suddenly full of tears. "Why not?"

"I'm afraid. What if I break it? What if it doesn't sound the same?" Lyra asked. I handed the harp back to her. "Do you think Mom would want me to?"

"If it breaks, I'm sure Icarus will rebuild it even stronger. If it doesn't sound the same, he could fix that too," I responded, taking a steadying breath. "Mom loved it when you played. She got you the harp because she knew you would adore it. If she were here now, she'd ask you to play, but only if you wanted to. If you don't want to play it, you don't have to. It is yours—your gift. Use it how you want."

"You don't use your gift," Lyra said as she took the harp back.

"What are you talking about? I use my gift of truth all the time. Our angel gifts are different from that harp," I responded.

Lyra leaned close and whispered, "You never use

your angel-light or angel—" She stumbled over naming my third gift, a side effect of the only angel-bond my mother intentionally put on us. To protect us both, no one could know about my third gift.

"Those are dangerous. They hurt people. They don't help. I could get in a lot of trouble if angels knew what I can do," I whispered back. "You haven't told anyone, have you?"

"No, but Icarus was curious," Lyra responded.

"I bet he was," I said dryly. "Are you happy here? I have a job to finish, but then we can move anywhere. Go anywhere." I ignored an unwelcome pang in my chest at the idea of walking away from a certain tall, fierce, and passionate archangel.

"I don't want to leave. I just got here," Lyra responded immediately, clearly upset.

"Ladies, I'm back," Rachiel called from the doorway as she placed a serving tray of three steaming mugs. I rose from the settee and took two cups from her. I handed one to Lyra, and she took it gratefully.

"How often do events like this happen?" I asked Rachiel.

She set her tray down, then picked up the last mug for herself before sitting in a chair next to us. I sipped the melted chocolate. It was divine. The indulgent creamy, chocolate drink was equally comforting and a pick me up I desperately needed. Exhaustion played at the edges of my mind, and sleep beckoned me.

"To be frank, the last time the city rose up against the angels was when the House of Lords arrested your father. Many of us did not agree with the verdict," Rachiel said. "Before that, it was usually only small demon uprisings. That a faction has grown so strong to threaten us all is concerning, but the Viscount seems to have it in hand."

A bell sounded far off; the noise grew louder until Rachiel rose from her seat. She set her mug down suddenly, the drink sloshing over the sides as she strode toward the sounds. "Excuse me, ladies."

In the distance, I heard doors opening and slamming shut. I downed the rest of my chocolate, wishing it was something a bit more stimulating. "Something isn't right," I whispered to Lyra. "We need to go."

"I haven't finished my drink, and Miss Rachiel will be right back," Lyra responded.

"Finish it or bring it with you. We are leaving now. At least find somewhere to hide. Where are the others?" I asked. Lyra scowled, but quickly drank the rest of her beverage and rose from the couch.

"They're upstairs, near the roof where their parents are fetching them. Anyone staying is either raiding the kitchen or in bed," Lyra explained.

"Then we need to go to the kitchen. Is there a back door?" I asked. Lyra shook her head and skirted her way behind me. Her eyes widened as she looked at the door, causing me to look in that direction.

"Leaving so soon, Nora?" a familiar masculine voice questioned from the parlor doorway. "You just got here."

"Baron Mercer, what are you doing here?" I asked, and shoved Lyra further behind me. Mercer smiled.

"Kassian sent me to check in on you." The lie slid over my skin like rough sandpaper. It tasted sour and set me on edge.

"I think we both know that's not true," I responded.

"Isn't it?" Mercer grinned as alarms began to sound and security lights flashed.

CHAPTER 16

Lyra's hands gripped the back of my chain mail tightly. I felt as she pressed herself against my back, then as she pressed a worn handle into my palm. It was the knife I had given her for her tenth birthday to defend herself if need be.

"Is that your sister?" Mercer asked, his voice booming over the alarms.

"That's none of your business. You shouldn't be here, Mercer. What are you up to?" I asked coolly. He shook his head and approached a bookcase across from him. He moved the bust of some old angel revealing a keypad. He entered a code, and the alarms stopped, and the lights ceased their flashing. He tossed the bust back and forth between his hands like a ball.

"That's better," Mercer murmured. "Is that your sister?"

"Lyra, go. Get out of here, join the others and get out," I whispered to her.

"What about you?" she asked.

"I'll catch up," I responded, even as the archangel

glared at me. Lyra's hands fell away from my back. I heard her as she turned and ran for the back door out of the parlor. "What are you doing here, Mercer?"

"I'm here to take care of you and your sister," Mercer said, and this time it was not a lie.

"Why?"

"You're valuable to me." Again, the truth. "Angels with the power of angel-light are rare, rarer still after so many tried to close the gate and failed. Almost as rare as angels with angel-flame, like Kassian. Your father succeeded where others failed."

"So I've been told," I responded as he moved around the room, each step bringing him closer. I stayed between him and the door, blocking his path to follow Lyra. "We don't have angel-light," I responded. "That's an archangel gift."

"Even if you don't, the demons don't know that," Mercer said with a wicked smile. "Without your father around to unlock the gate, they want you and your sister. They'll burn this city to the ground to get what they want."

"The school is warded. They can't get in." I hoped that was the truth, as my thoughts went to the students left here.

"The school is warded," Mercer parroted, the lie sickly sweet in the air. My stomach rolled at the stench. "It was until I broke it. For all her gifts and secrets, Helena's blood is the key to half the city's wards."

"Kassian will come. He'll kill you for this betrayal," I said. Mercer threw the bust at me suddenly. I ducked, and it hit the wall behind me, bursting into a cloud of stone and dust.

"How do you know Kassian didn't orchestrate this

entire event to gain complete control over the city?" Mercer asked. "He has a king's power, the power of fire. He could easily light the entire city ablaze in a fit of rage if the mood struck him."

"He cares about the city. He wouldn't torch everything," I said as I moved away from Mercer, stepping closer to the door Lyra had exited through. I barely knew Kassian, but he seemed to value the city and life more than I ever expected an angel to. He valued me. That had to count for something. Didn't it?

"Kassian is a fool! He could renounce his position as Viscount of this city, claim his mate, and be king with his bloodline and powers, but he refuses! He wants to save the city. Arcadia needs saving! Arcadia has been without a king for generations, even though Kassian has the angel-fire to rule. They would welcome him back with open arms if only he would give up this forsaken city and stand with the House instead of against it so often," Mercer hissed. "If only he would give up lost causes like you!"

"Maybe he will one day," I quipped. I wasn't naïve. Kassian and I had a connection, and he was an amazing lover, but a man like him didn't settle for a halfling like me. Heir to the kingdom or not, we were unmatched and nearly strangers. Well acquainted with each other's bodies, but strangers nonetheless. Mercer laughed cruelly as I stood my ground and gripped my small knife.

"He will be too late. By then, the gate to hell will be open. A new king will emerge from the fires to take his place," Mercer responded. "This city is lost. This world will fall to darkness and flame. Then, Arcadia will tremble as their new king reigns."

"It won't happen," I argued. The idea of a king born

of hell was terrifying. East End still bore the scars of the damage demons wrought on the city unchecked before the angels rescued the humans. If a king rose from hell, humanity would be lost and the demons would make sure of it.

"Foolish woman, it already is," Mercer sneered as he moved further away from me. His hand went to the keypad on the wall again. "Coming for you and your sister is the first step, and you aren't the only ones we're coming for. As the city burns, demons are collecting all the legacy angels they can get their hands on—bastards, purebloods, and even halflings—to open the gate."

"If the demons are doing your dirty work, then why are you here?" I hissed as I stepped closer to Mercer. He smiled darkly as his hand hovered over the keypad.

"To see the job done and to open the door," Mercer purred as he pushed a button on the keypad nestled into the bookcase. From the hall, I heard the click of locks unraveling. I moved back to block Lyra's exit. My eyes locked on Mercer until I looked over his shoulder and saw through the entrance into the room. On the floor, with blood pooling beneath her, laid Rachiel, unmoving. A knife stuck out from her back between her damaged wings.

I heard heavy doors swing open, similar to the sound of the front doors I had come through earlier. Sounds of growls echoed in the air. I saw demons covered in fur with fangs and claws stalk into the hallway on two legs through the doorway. The beasts were hellhounds—demon werewolf offspring. I had never seen one outside of the demon sector before. The hellhounds' fur was the color of slate, some of their fangs longer than my fingers, and they weren't alone. More demons crowded in behind them, fire demons and vampires. The rest I didn't recognize. I didn't want to meet any of them up close, either. One demon was bad, but a dozen? This school would be in ruins by dawn.

"You're late," Mercer yelled over his shoulder. Through the doorway, I saw the demon in charge snapped his head in our direction as the others spread out and took off running in different directions.

"Sorry, boss, angels kept us busy," the demon hissed, his trench-coat swaying with each step. "Is this the girl?"

"One of them," Mercer said.

"She doesn't look like much," the demon hissed.

"She's a halfling, but you'd recognize her father if you met him," Mercer said with a frown. "Her brat of a sister ran that way. Remember, we want them alive."

"I'll get her," the demon responded.

"You'll do no such thing," I growled. "Go back where you came from."

Both the demon and Mercer laughed. The demon approached me slowly. His skin was pale but mottled with black veins and splotches. His nails were filed to points and glinted like metal. A goblin demon, their love of coins literally consumed them. Humans once, until they died and were reborn from their own greed. They consumed metal until they became what they loved and turned into an immovable mass of metal and toxins. Mercer and the demon were quite the pair.

"Do you need her unharmed?" the goblin asked as he sized me up. The sound of screams, growls, and fighting echoed down the halls of the school. I hazarded a quick glance at the door behind me. The path Lyra took was silent; I wasn't sure if that was a good sign or not. I gripped my knife tightly as tension coursed through my body. I needed a plan to get out of here and follow her. My sister needed me; fuck archangels and their power plays.

"Mostly," Mercer said.

The goblin didn't hesitate. He rushed me. His violet eyes focused, his claws reaching for my face. I dodged the wicked claws as Mercer watched from the sidelines. I thrust my knife out and plunged it deep into the demon's abdomen. Thick, hot, black blood rushed from the wound over my hand. It burned worse than any chemical burn I'd ever encountered. I pulled my knife free, but was forced to drop it as the demon hissed. The blade was almost gone, eroded by the demon's body. The demon rushed me again, his arms flailing, coat flapping behind him. One hand caught me across the face, and three lines of pain erupted across my cheek as he tackled me to the ground.

"Remember, keep her alive," Mercer murmured as he walked past to the now unguarded door, likely in search of Lyra. The demon grunted and continued trying to claw at my face as I struggled and tried to throw him off. "At least until we have her sister."

Rage stirred in my blood. Fury and fear burning bright for my sister, for myself. These bastards would not do this to us, not now. Not when my sister and I were on the path to brighter, happier days. I screamed in rage and grabbed the demon's face instead of defending my own. I pressed my thumbs into his eyes until his screams were louder than my own. My hands grew hot where they came into contact with his skin, but instead of burning with acidic fervor, they began to glow. The same glow that had unleashed itself when

Kassian brought me to the edge of euphoria. This time, my glow was pure rage made light.

The demon fought to free himself from my grasp. He screamed louder as his skin hardened before turning to ash beneath my palms. He thrashed, but I held on, heedless of the cuts and slashes he wrought until the demon went slack. From what I could tell, half his body appeared to be a burned log and dead coals. I pushed the goblin demon's body off mine and scrambled to my feet.

One down, a dozen to go, and one goddamned archangel that would regret ever messing with the halfling sisters of East End. If Lyra and I could make it to dawn, we would be safe. Sunlight drained most demons of their powers and killed weaker ones. The demons would have to crawl back into whatever hell they crawled out of if they wanted to survive to fight another night. I needed a weapon, and the parlor offered little in the way of armaments beyond books. I walked to one of the antique end tables, flipped it over, and snapped off two table legs—they would have to do. A scream made my blood run cold for a moment. It came from the direction Lyra had run.

"Nora!!!" Lyra's voice echoed in fear throughout the halls.

"Lyra!" I roared and ran through the door to meet the nightmare that awaited me.

CHAPTER 17

The screams of multiple children pulled at my soul. I passed more than one struggle between an adult and a demon, but no children. The teachers left at the small boarding school had risen up to fight back, but were woefully outnumbered. The angel stronghold was quickly becoming a battlefield of debris, bodies, and injured. I didn't stop running, even as smoke spread into the hallway. I followed the screams, even though I no longer heard Lyra.

"Lyra!" I yelled. A hellhound stepped out of the room and into my path in the hall, blood soaked its muzzle. It growled as it focused its gaze on me. I tightened my grip on the broken table legs I wielded. It snarled, dropped to four legs, and charged me. It snapped its jaws as it gained speed. The hellhound clearly did not get Mercer's *do not kill angels* memo or at least thought it didn't apply to me. It lunged for my throat. I thrust one table leg between its fangs while swinging to hit the beast in the ribs with the other. The hellhound still knocked me to the ground. It continued to snap at me around the wood. I dropped one makeshift club to keep the other firmly between its fangs. It growled, clenched the wood between its teeth, and wrenched it away; bloody foam bubbled from its muzzle. Its eyes were bloodshot and wild as the hellhound howled.

I scrambled back from it as quickly as I could, trying to find my other makeshift weapon. My hand gripped the old wood and turned it toward the hellhound's chest as the beast lunged. Its fangs sunk deep into my shoulder, causing pain to radiate through my body as its fangs cut through the chain mail and bone crunched beneath the force. A scream ripped from my body as the hellhound whined. For a moment, it tightened its hold on me and shook his head, attempting to maul me further. I pushed the makeshift stake deeper into the hound's body before letting go and putting my hands on his muzzle. I let the rage in my soul bubble and burst through my hands. The wolf yelped and jerked away immediately, but the damage was done.

The hellhound sagged on the floor. Its breathing became labored, and its muzzle and face were covered in the same burned ember pattern as the goblin demon.

"Lyra!" I yelled, and struggled to my feet. I tugged the broken chain mail out of my wounded shoulder, then lumbered over to the dying hellhound. I yanked the blood-soaked table leg from its chest and watched as blood gushed from the wound. The hellhound stopped breathing. "Lyra!"

"Nora!!! Nora, I'm here!" Lyra's voice rang out, closer than before. I ran, my blood leaving a path behind me. The half dozen demons I encountered either got a table leg to the head or a burning handprint before I reached the doors of the kitchen. The sight there made my blood boil.

Huddled in the corner was Lyra, with six other young angels. Opposite them were Mercer and two vampires. The angels stood between Lyra and Mercer. They formed a protective barrier in front of their newest friend. I recognized the moment Lyra saw me. Her eyes widened, but she didn't utter a word as I silently stalked behind the closest vampire. I thrust the table leg into his back without hesitation. His body turned to ash in my hands before he could even make a sound. The second vampire turned to me and hissed. Mercer cussed and lunged for the children. One angel formed a shield around the group that Mercer couldn't break, and he responded with another cuss.

"Restrain that one if you can, otherwise kill her and we'll make do without her. She's not worth the trouble," Mercer ordered the vampire as he pointed at me. He was furious, veins popping with tension in his forehead and neck.

"Gladly," the vampire said.

"No! Nora! Don't hurt her!" Lyra screamed.

"Lyra, run! Take the others and go! I'll be fine!"

"She's lying. Look at her, Lyra, she's injured. We will kill her unless you come with us," Mercer said. He recognized the opportunity for what it was, and I was furious. There was nothing I could do until I dealt with the vampire staring me down.

"Lyra, go. Don't listen to him. He's a liar! You can't trust him. You can't trust the archangels. Run now, we have friends who can help. Find Micheal or Oliva, you know who to trust. Go!" I ordered, when Lyra looked back at me with hesitation.

"I'll make you a deal, Lyra," Mercer purred and Lyra

turned that innocent fear stricken gaze back on the archangel with a glimmer of hope. Black hate for him seethed in the deepest parts of my soul. How dare he try to make a deal with my sister?

"No!" I roared as the vampire threw a series of punches at me. The children screamed as Mercer attempted to force his hand through their shield. It wavered as he tried to transform it into something else with his angel power.

"Lyra, don't you dare take a deal from that angel!" I yelled as I evaded the vampire's next hit. He swung punch after punch, hook after hook, his fangs dripping with excitement.

"Lyra, make a deal, or your sister dies," Mercer threatened as the vampire landed a punch to my stomach. I growled.

"No!" I said and thrust my hand into the vampire's face. Light burst from my hand, and the vampire screeched. Some of the angel children gasped. A door behind the children was wrenched open where they hadn't thought to form a shield.

There, in the shadow of the kitchen, stood Silas. His eyes blazed as he saw the vampire turn to ash at my feet, but he didn't say a word. He looked between Mercer and me, his eyes full of distrust.

What are you up to, girl? Silas whispered against my mind. His wings flared behind him. The smoke seemed to move around him as if he was part of it—his shadow-gift. *Don't tell me you're a part of this. Kassian is coming.*

I'm only here for my sister. I spoke to Silas, hoping he could read my mind. *Protect my sister halfling, protect her as if your soul depended on it.* His nod was all the confirmation I needed, though I would have felt better if I could have made him swear on it. There was no time. I had to trust Silas now and deal with the consequences. Silas reached out, grabbed Lyra by the shoulder, even as Mercer protested, and pulled her through the doorway leading outside. The rest of her angel friends followed, disappearing into the dawning light.

The fear for my sister's safety eased some now that she was no longer cornered by Mercer. The lack of fear made way for the mounting rage at the archangel. We wouldn't be safe if Mercer kept coming for us. He needed to die.

"Like father, like daughter. Always causing trouble, never leaving well enough alone, and keeping secrets. You have angel-light," Mercer said as he turned to me. Rage colored his cheeks as he rolled up his sleeves. "You'll regret this, girl."

"What are you going to do about it?" I quipped.

"Teach you not to meddle in the affairs of Arcadia and hell. A rightful king is coming. You don't want to stand in his path," Mercer threatened, before picking up a simple kitchen blade. "Without your sister, I need you alive, but only long enough to get what we need to open the gate."

Before my eyes, the chef's knife transformed into a honed, elaborate board sword reminiscent of the weapons shown in the mural at the House of Lords. My table leg was a sorry, battered excuse for a weapon in comparison. My strong arm was already damaged by the hellhound. This would not go well.

"You know, I don't understand you. You were willing to sell your blood before. You were willing to make a deal with Kassian. You're so desperate to rise above your place in this city, but chose not to make a deal with me?" Mercer asked. "A deal with me is much more profitable than warming Kassian's bed. I can still make all your problems go away."

"I'm easy to understand. I do everything for my sister. Everything I do, I do for her," I responded. Mercer scoffed and behind him, demons approached. They crowded the hallway, hesitantly entering the ashen kitchen, and stood at their leader's back.

"How noble for a halfling. I doubt even your soul would amount to much. You'll never ascend to a full angel, never gain wings, no matter what passing power you have," Mercer mocked. "No matter what you barter away in her name."

"Silas has wings," I responded. Mercer laughed.

"Is that what you truly desire? Wings? How human," Mercer sneered.

I gritted my teeth as the demons crept closer, even though a pang of pain echoed in my heart. I had dreamed of flying for years, of wings appearing one day and soaring beside my father, until my mother explained it was an impossibility. That he was never ever coming back, and I would never mature and ascend into a full angel.

"Silas is half archangel, half archdemon. He has the ability to control half the creatures of the Pit with a thought. You're nothing. Your power is nothing but a fancy light show. You'll never have wings, never know your true mate. Your human heart will hold you down. You and your sister should have stayed down where you belonged instead of stepping foot in the Tower. The shadows hid you, protected you. Archangel Ramiel's daughters were a mere whispered rumor until word of the auction spread," Mercer said. "Your own greed was your undoing."

"You, girl, you lit the match that is burning the city.

When the demons heard not one, but both of Ramiel's daughters were in the city, they were eager to make a deal to free their leader." Mercer laughed as he moved closer with the blade in his hand. "Throughout his questioning, Ramiel swore his daughters would bring light to the world, that you were the future. He was right, in a way; you lit the city on fire."

Mercer made his move as his lackeys snarled at my back. I gripped the table leg like a baseball bat even as my shoulder screamed in protest, just as I heard glass shatter in the distance. Mercer lunged at me and swung the sword with a speed I hadn't expected. His wings materialized, followed by a chest plate over his suit. I ducked, evaded, or blocked each strike again and again. He grinned, merely playing with me.

"I really should thank you. Because of you, the new king will rise. I'll be at his side and the House will fall. The Commons will be destroyed, and I will get what I am owed. Lucifer will see to it," Mercer said. He swung again; this time, the table leg split in two. The blade continued its path downward, straight for my injured and exposed shoulder.

Another blade intercepted the sword as it swung toward me. Sparks flashed as I was shoved roughly backward toward the door Lyra had fled through. Burgundy wings shielded me as Kassian stood between Mercer and me.

"Uncle, what is the meaning of this?" Kassian yelled and pushed Mercer back. "What are you doing here?"

"That woman betrayed us. I want her head!" Mercer responded. "She broke into the school and caused the wards to fail. She opened the school to the demons. They're here for the children; most of the teachers are slain! Rachiel is gone."

The demons stood behind Mercer calmly, without interceding on my behalf or his. The demons that Mercer was more than comfortable showing his back to. That lying fucking bastard.

"Why are you here and not defending the House?" Kassian asked coolly. "Rachiel let Nora in because I told her to. Nora didn't have access to unlock the school, so I brought her myself."

"Then you're a fool. She's tricked you. She's been lying to you," Mercer said.

"Is that so?" Kassian asked curiously.

"She has angel-light. She's made a pact with the demons," Mercer said. Before I could utter a word in my defense, Kassian whirled around with a frown on his face and put his sword to my throat. The demons didn't move a muscle.

"Go, now!" Kassian commanded. "That's an order, Nora. A deal has been struck; a deal must be honored," he reminded me, as if the tingling of the angel enchantment across my shoulders wasn't enough. I had to follow his every order, his every command, even as my soul raged. Burning erupted across my back, mingling with the pain. Kassian watched as I stepped back toward the open door.

"I can't let her go," Mercer snarled. I looked back as Mercer swung his sword into Kassian's unprotected wings. Kassian's anguished cry as he fell to his knees from the blow seared my soul. Bloody burgundy feathers fell to the ground around him, the red atrocity vibrant against the white kitchen tiles. Mercer swung his sword again. Kassian blocked it as flames covered his wings. His eyes became embers as he staggered to his feet while pushing back against the man he called uncle. He was an avenging archangel of flame and fury.

"You're making a mistake," Mercer muttered and swung again. Kassian blocked once more. "She is the key. She is the reason the city burns."

Kassian was beyond words. He merely growled. He was becoming overcome with rage—angel-rage. Mercer's eyes widened.

"You gave me no choice, nephew," Mercer whispered. He picked up half of what remained of my broken table leg. The leg transformed into a gleaming knife made of wood and metal. Lost to rage, Kassian didn't see it. Unprotected, as I wore Kassian's armor, the blade easily pierced Kassian's torso. It was a minor wound, but it was enough to distract him from his killing rage. Kassian stepped back, looking at the wood and metal blade. He grunted and stumbled to his knees. His sword fell from his hands as they went to his stomach. Focused on the wound now, he didn't see Mercer's sword.

"Say hello to your father in the afterlife," Mercer whispered, and swung his sword again.

CHAPTER 18

Faster than I've ever moved before, I ran as if I was light myself. Every moment slowed down. I put myself in front of Kassian as a shield, standing over his broken form. I was a daughter of light, but I was born in secret shadows. Rage burned beneath my skin. The angel enchantment seared my shoulders as I disobeyed Kassian's order. The pain only fueled my rage. A dark anger that would burn everything it touched until only light remained—Mercer would be no exception.

Mercer's blade came closer, but I would not go peacefully into the shadows even if he killed me in the process. My father was right; I would bring the light. I could only hope that it would heal Kassian in time, like it had healed my mother and sister years ago. I could only hope that Lyra would be safe and that Kassian would keep his end of the deal. I had uncovered the traitor, after all.

Angel-rage consumed me as the blade made

contact. Mercer's eyes went wide before he turned to shield himself from the damage he had unwittingly unleashed. I screamed as light erupted from my palms, from the killing blow, then my entire body. Inside the dark, demolished kitchen, I became a beacon of light with such force the world became nothing but white.

As the light hit the demons, they turned to ash. The power behind the light threw Mercer back against the wall. I heard Kassian collapse and groan behind me. For a moment, everything was peaceful in the light, the darkness thrown back out of reach. The light wrapped around me in a safe embrace, as if I had wings, as if I were flying above the city in the peace of night in Kassian's arms.

Pain. Pain ripped along my back. The broken deal had come to collect its due—pain everywhere. It consumed me until nothing but darkness remained, stripped of all light. To the darkness, I succumbed.

I was born in the shadows of the city, a daughter of light.

The darkness rushed up to consume me.

This time, I dreamed of flying in the dawn, rising from the shadows.

Death was cold, dark, smelled of mildew, and was excruciatingly painful. I noticed the sound of someone pacing near me almost immediately. My body felt heavy, weak, and weighed down. Sounds became clearer as the hazy pain subsided, though I wish they hadn't. Muffled screams and growls surrounded me. I opened my eyes to see what death looked like. A cell. A set of chains encompassed my wrists. Dark slate concrete walls, pitted with claw marks and scarred with tally marks.

"Good, you're awake," a husky voice said stiffly. "That took longer than expected, but it was the best the angel could do. Apparently, it's not exactly easy to find a healer right now."

"Who's there?" I asked, my voice hoarse. The stranger stayed in the shadows, out of sight.

"I'll ask the questions," the voice murmured from the shadows. "First, tell me why an archangel pulled me out of solitary confinement to babysit a fledgling? Who are *you*?"

"I'm no one, just a halfling," I said. The mystery man grunted at my response.

"We both know that's not true," the man responded. "They allowed you to be bandaged up, shoulder, neck, and back. Yet they still insisted on putting you in those damned chains."

"Who are they? Where am I?" I asked as dread settled hard in my stomach. "I'm not dead." The man laughed.

"That would be a kinder fate than this hellhole. The House of Lords insisted on the chains," the man said sadly. "An archangel has taken steps to heal you, to protect you, and to place us in solitary together for now. You're in the Pit and I want to know what in the name of Arcadia you did to end up here." Hope grew in my heart. An archangel looked after me. Maybe Kassian lived. Footsteps grew louder as the man walked closer. "There are whispers of a halfling that made a deal with the Viscount. The same halfling started a revolution to free demons and their king. That a halfling betrayed a school of angel children to a demon horde for coin. There are whispers of a halfling that turned night into day and destroyed every demon within five city blocks. A halfling with angel-light powers this world has never seen," the voice said, getting louder and more agitated. "They accused the same halfling of attempting to kill Viscount Kassian Oriel, the true heir to the Arcadia throne and his Uncle Baron Mercurial. Rumors suggest that if the Viscount isn't already dead, he will be soon. You will be put on trial soon for these crimes. Baron Mercurial stands as the only living witness to the events."

"No! It's a lie! I protected Kassian. Mercer is a traitor!" I yelled as my heart broke for what could have been. What was lost. Kassian was dying, or dead. I didn't heal him, but if he didn't look out for me, who did?

"Yet, that isn't all, and this is where it gets interesting," the voice murmured. "I saw your injuries. I bandaged them myself. Your shoulder is a parting gift from a hellhound bite, your neck is from an archangel blade, you're covered in poisoned goblin cuts, but your back—you've sprouted wings, halfling. You've ascended."

"Halflings don't ascend," I parroted Mercer's words. I desperately wanted to see what the man was talking about. Even if I could get the bandage off, there would be no way for me to see my back in this dingy cell.

"No, they don't. Not until now. I'm here to help you and your sister wherever she may be."

"Lyra? What happened?" I asked as I struggled to my feet, even with my hands chained together in front of me, only to fall back to the ground as the world seemed to sway and shift beneath my feet.

"Rumor has it she disappeared into the shadows of the city with a flock of angel children under her spell, courtesy of her angel-song gift," the man said. "The House of Lords is searching building by building, at least the ones left standing."

"No, Silas was supposed to protect her," I whispered. My bruised heart grieved; it was all for naught. Kassian and Lyra were in danger. I was stuck in the Pit, a failure.

"I need answers, Nora. You know you can't lie to me, daughter." I snapped my head toward the voice. Vivid green eyes stared back at me, eyes I thought I'd never see again. The angel stepped out of the shadows. He towered over me, his wings flared at his back. Once they had been emerald green, now they were as black as pure ebony. Like he had done so many times in my memories and my dreams, he squatted in front of me until he was looking me in the eye.

"We have a lot to get caught up on, Nora," my father said as he reached out and took my hand. "I'm getting you out of these chains and out of this prison before your trial, if it's the last thing I do. I've already lost your mother. I'm not losing you and your sister to that bastard's machinations."

"You're alive? But... how?" I whispered. "Mom—" I choked on the words, that I couldn't save her.

"Protected you the best she could until she died, almost two months ago," father said softly, grief coloring his words.

"How do you know?" I asked. His green eyes sought mine.

"I felt it the moment she passed. I felt her soul

leave. My wings turned black in mourning for my true mate," Ramiel said with a soft smile. "A human mate with a heart of gold and the mother of my children. She brought more light to my life than I could have imagined."

"I'm sorry I couldn't heal her. If I had known you were alive, I would have brought her to you. Your angel-light could have healed her," I said.

Ramiel shook his head.

"An angel's light can only heal a person once, and never one's own mate," my father explained. "No one could have saved your mother. That was never your burden to bear. What do you say we get you out of these cuffs?"

"Please," I said.

Ramiel cussed.

"These aren't designed to come off easily. This is going to hurt, unfortunately. I don't have Icarus's skill, but he taught me a few tricks over the years. You'll likely pass out again. Are you sure?" Ramiel asked.

"I can handle it," I asserted stiffly, and braced myself. My father only softly chuckled in response.

"I'm sure. Maybe you can help me with something I haven't quite figured out yet," Ramiel said.

"What?"

"Why do your fledgling wings appear to match the wings of a certain would-be king archangel that dropped me into the Pit in the first place?" Ramiel asked as he wrenched my cuffs. Something snapped in my wrists before blinding pain overwhelmed me.

Continue the Archangel's Legacy Series in book two,
The Archangel's Mate.
Coming Soon in 2023
Sign up here for updates:
https://newsletter.kreaauthor.com/

ACKNOWLEDGMENTS

Cover & Interior Graphics by
| DoElle Designs |
www.doelledesigns.com

Editing by
|CamRei Editing|
https://www.facebook.com/CamRei.Editing
&
|Fluffy Fox Editing|
https://fluffyfoxllc.wixsite.com/fluffyfoxpublishing

Formatting by
| Kreative-Books, LLC |

SPECIAL THANKS

First, thank you to my family for their continued support.

Second thank you to my editors and beta readers; Amanda, Jes, Torri, Quell, Jes, and Sara–working with you all has been a delight. This story would not have been the same without your input and sass. <3

Third, thank you to my readers–thank you for reading this far and coming on this journey with me. There are more books to come!!!

Last but most of all, my kids. Thank you Ellie, for being my shining star lighting up my world day after day. Baby Wy, you were there every step of the way for this novel though you probably approved more of the playlist than the story, thank you for all the kicks. You've both flipped my world upside down so many times but I know one thing for sure - I love you both. You're amazing kids.

ABOUT THE AUTHOR

K. Rea lives in Florida with her family and two rescue fur-babies. She is a part-time paranormal romance writer of fated mates, rejected mates, fairytale retellings and enemies to lovers tropes. If she's not living life to the fullest or writing, you'd probably find her with her nose in a book enjoying a lukewarm cup of coffee.

Sign Up to K. Rea's Newsletter or
Follow her on Social Media for Updates!

Newsletter | https://kreaauthor.com/
Instagram | https://www.instagram.com/krea_author/
Bookbub | https://www.bookbub.com/profile/k-rea
Twitter | https://twitter.com/krea_author

Printed in Great Britain
by Amazon